SPONTA

RECKLESS

By

E. Ellen

DEDICATION

*This book is dedicated to my husband who supported me
regardless of thinking I was writing about secret love affairs.
I truly love your sense of humour.
Also to my four children who allowed my spare time to be
filled scribbling notes.*

CONTENTS

ACKNOWLEDGMENTS

Thanks to Jason for allowing me to have time out to raise our four gorgeous children, where I found the time to find this dream. You are my best friend, my soulmate and my true inspiration and without you I would not believe in myself. I thank you for allowing me to find my true passion where my naughty thoughts finally made it from pen to paper.

For my family and friends who spurred me on, read my notes, my first copies and gave me the honest feedback I needed. Without those wanting to read it publishing would still be fantasy.

Thank you to those who do not know who they are, who helped build my characters.

Finally thank you to those who read my book. I hope it brings you the strength to overcome those emotional rollercoasters life throws at you. Enjoy.

CHAPTER 1

Mr Jones

The alarm beeped loudly for what felt like the tenth time. She gave it a quick hit and finally gave in to the day ahead. Her eyes opened, feeling less heavy than the night before following several late nights of dusting off ends of assignments ready for those all-important final deadlines.

"Oh shit, shit, shit!" she exclaimed as she notices the time. "I'm late!" She jumped up, throwing off her purple silk quilt revealing her sun-kissed curvy body in nothing put a pair of girl boxers and an oversized t-shirt. Rushing out of bed, she grabbed the cleanest pair of tight gym leggings, sports bra and top, making herself presentable for her day at university. Stumbling about her bedroom she quickly brushed her teeth as she glanced in the mirror, pleased she decided to shower last night.

She ran down the stairs; perching on the bottom step, she pulled on her loosely tied trainers, grabbed her bag, locked the door and made her way to her car. On the 24-minute drive over to University she quickly applies a flick of eyeliner and a smidge of shiny lip gloss, making her feel fit to be seen at her first lecture. Her long, thick, brown hair hand brushed on the way through the campus door, with its natural wave falls down her back, getting caught in her heavy bag strap. Eager for the days of carrying so many folders, books and laptop around to be over, she was counting down the days till graduation when her shoulder ache would start to ease. As she pulled at the strap to remove the uncomfortable strain on her hair she got herself in a tizzy, entwining her bag and iPhone headphones, her hair now all over the place. Whilst rushing up the stairs with no time to stop, she became aggravated, hating the fact she was rushing and now flustered. Why did the sports classrooms have to be on the top floor?

The newly built campus consisted of four storeys and a large spacious layout, each floor overlooking the other over the indoor balconies completed with large windows letting plenty of light in. The great white walls were complemented by purple and green furniture which she liked as green was her favourite colour. Several libraries were found, each containing the old and newest specific books for each subjects which she used daily rather than buying every recommended book to get her through her assignments. From the fourth floor she could admire the green surroundings of the football pitch where the sports lads would spend most of their time; benches would fill with the beauty students to eye up their muscular bodies most lunchtimes. Obviously she also had a look every now and again. On the bottom floor she spent her time spending money in the onsite Costa where she came to favour a caramel hot chocolate whenever she was feeling cold. The only dislike she found within her surroundings was the lifts, which were only for the use of lecturers and those with authorisation, resulting in the last three years of climbing four flights of stairs to become the norm. Although she had found this had helped tone her buttocks quite a bit.

"Here, let me help you." A gentle but manly voice came her way as she felt the weight of her bag strap being lifted by the stranger behind her. Turning towards her oncomer, she was knocked back a few steps as she set her gaze into the dark green eyes of her gorgeous and favourite lecturer, Mr Matt Jones. He stood before her in his usual sports attire, a polo shirt along with his shorts, allowing his athlete thighs to be on show which she enjoyed thoroughly. His dark brown hair was left to fall naturally which he often brushed to the side, complemented by his smoothly shaved face with a slight sign of aging beginning to show around his eyes.

"Err, thanks," she responded with a nervous smile as she sorted herself out, trying not to blush at the sight of him.

"You're late this morning, Miss Bell, let's get a move on," he urged with a grin. "I am looking forward to your assessment this afternoon, I hope you're ready." Placing further pressure onto her; she was already dreading it due to her pure hatred of roleplay assessments.

"I think so, I can't say I am looking forward to it though," she mumbled.

She asked herself, why would anyone look forward to performing a physical assessment on one of the hottest men they know in order to pass their degree?

Just why? Why did there have to be a lack of students on her course?

In a large sports room equipped with the latest sports science gizmos and gadgets sat a handful of students mainly consisting of immature late-teen-years boys, and one normal mid-twenty-something lad; there was no sign of another female among the course other than a lecturer who each of the boys gawked upon as she roamed the halls in her tight leggings. It came as no surprise to her that she was the going to be one of the oldest students due to deciding late what she wanted to do with her career, although she did wish there were more females to talk to. With no desire to chat to anyone in sight, sitting and staring at the muscular body of the sports teacher Mr Jones, which she had ogled for the past three years, was the only option.

"Freya, Freya? Miss Bell!" Mr Jones exclaimed, pulling out her headphones, taking her away from her distractingly loud Maroon 5 album which she appeared to have zoned out to. She stared at his small rose-coloured lips as he spoke, looking up at him standing above her, his tanned face becoming a distraction from what he was actually saying. His eyes started to squint further as his frown grew, acknowledging she was still not listening.

"Uh-hum?"

"I hope you will be more focused within your assessment than what you are currently," he snapped.

"Yes, sorry sir, I am just a bit... distracted."

"For the thousandth time, Freya, the term's nearly over, when are you going to call me Matt like I've asked? You make me feel old." He turned his back to her and walked towards the front of the room as she sat up straight, turning her music off as she watched his every move, nibbling her lip.

Ouch. A harsh reminder of her upcoming graduation stung like a bee, knowing once it was over she would never get to look upon the fine specimen of a man whom she had spent the last three years daydreaming about. Being only two years older than her at a young age of 27, appearing single, although probably not and quite obviously somewhat of her type, she often hated obeying the rules of teacher and student romances which had stopped her giving into her usual flirting behaviour for so long. Anyone else she would have fucked senseless numerous times by now. The intense feelings and appalling naughty thoughts which penetrated her mind and body felt soul destroying as they could never be truly satisfied. For this reason she had found herself fulfilling her aching loins with one-night stands every other weekend. Admittedly she had somehow fallen into the student lifestyle she said she never would with no intention of changing it.

As she finished off her tuna pasta pot and fruit, took a sip of her water and eyed up her iWatch, nerves swirled her stomach as she had to make her way to her final assessment which she had been fearing all week. Her assessment consisted of performing a physical assessment on measuring body composition and due to the lack of students Matt had opted to be her acting client. Allowing her to see and touch his fine body made her hands shake, her chest thump and her lower extremities to become favourable. As she opened the door she could see he was already there chatting away with another of her lecturers; as they noticed her he made his way out the room.

"Good luck, Freya," he wished as he shut the door behind him, placing the 'assessment in progress' sign on the door. "Alright Freya, are we ready? What are we doing?" Mr Jones asked as he sat upon a workout bench almost looking as nervous as she felt. With everyone performing assessments this afternoon there was a schedule to abide by and it seemed he was eager to get straight into it. With no time to relax, she breathed in deeply, telling herself to control her hands and thoughts, and to keep them to herself. Mr Jones pushed play on the video camera as the recording began.

"In this assessment I am going to find out your body composition and body fat percentage by using the skinfold measurement method. I will need you to lift your shirt to allow me to take measurements of your upper body composition first from your biceps, pectorals and abdominal areas." As she looked up and down at him she swallowed deeply as she bit her inner lip, something she did every time she felt aroused. She shook her thoughts away and continued trying not to fluster. As she checked out his trim, toned body she felt flushed.

"As you are wearing shorts I can easily measure your thighs and calves," she shyly insisted.

Nervously giggling, she took hold of the apparatus and started to take measurements, her hands trembling.

She gently touched his body using nothing but her

fingertips, catching a glimpse of the way he was watching, her unsure of how to read his expression.

"To get a better reading, you will have to use more than just your fingertips. Don't worry, I don't bite," he whispered towards her. His comment made her gasp, she felt uncomfortable as she gripped more of his flesh as with his bold build there wasn't much to take hold of.

Whilst measuring his chest she felt his hand place upon her back, moving slowly towards her pert buttocks.

"If you get to touch me, it's only fair I get to do the same to you," he whispered in her ear. She paused, gazing into his come-to-bed eyes with complete shock as to what was happening.

Mr Jones pulled her close towards his chest, causing her to drop everything; he was unaware she was already ready for him, having had been for so long, plus the added thought of being caught caused her body to tremble with further excitement. He held her body tightly, placing his lips on hers for the first time. As she finally tasted him she furiously kissed him back, biting his lip as she let go. Turning him on even more, encouraging his cock to become large and solid against her body, he was giving her permission to do what she wanted after all this time. She took charge, pushing against him, making him sit upon the workout bench. Her thighs straddled him as they fiercely kissed, his hands upon her legs as they groped each other, both their bodies responding to each other's wants. She was ready for him, soaking wet and pulsing, waiting for his signal. He stood her up, undressing her rapidly from the waist down. Turning her around he bent her over and entered her with his thick cock pumping into her quickly; they fit together like a jigsaw.

His hands made their way under her sports bra stroking her large tits, arousing him more. He felt her erect nipples. *If only he could suck them,* she thought.

"I'm going to make you cum," he told her. Reaching his hand to her clit he circled it with the tip of his finger whilst the other hand stroked her breast as his dick thrusted hard into her. Her body tingling from head to toe, she was on edge of climax.

"Harder, deeper, come on," she moaned. He felt her tighten around his bulge, forcing him to pump aggressively. "Holy fuck!" she screamed whilst she came. He tugged at her long brown hair, feeling her juices, causing him to finish. Exiting her, he stood, taking a breath as he watched her turn, redressing herself. He gave her a beaming grin.

"What?" she asked.

"Well you passed that assessment with flying colours," he laughed. "You alright, Freya?" Mr Jones asked.

"Sorry, I lost my train of thought, can I start again?" she asked as she shook her dirty thoughts from her mind.

"Go on then, we don't have long though," he sighed with annoyance.

"Thank you." Second time round she held her hands stiff and got on with her assessment. *I'm going to need to go on a long run and a have cold shower when I get home,* she thought to herself. As the assessment finished she didn't stick around through pure embarrassment; she grabbed her bags and legged it to her car.

CHAPTER 2

Satisfied

As the sun sets outside she returns home from a six-mile run around the canal situated in a small village close by her home, a route which she favoured due to its change in incline and calm scenery. On a typical day she would observe dog walkers, barges moving along the water, couples dining on the outside decking of a busy restaurant, and families having picnics on the large surrounding fields. As she ran late this evening there was not much of an atmosphere but the quiet ambiances allowed her thoughts to now run clear. After a cool shower she threw on some comfy clothes ready for her chilled night in before her leaving party at work tomorrow evening. A chick flick and loads of chocolate with her three best mates.

Louise, aged 22, her hair generally straightened falls to her shoulders, a shade of brunette streaked by a pale blonde. Being the smallest of all of them all she stands at only five foot one, although her mouthy attitude makes up for this; she generally speaks her mind and enjoys a drink. She is the friend who will encourage Freya to go against her general behaviour as she loves a good story to tell. They have been best friends for life.

Nina, aged 27, being older than the others is perceived as the sensible one, not that age is a matter; this woman is of high intelligence, has never failed anything in her life and has a keen interest in getting her ducks in a row. She has been with the same guy since school. With gorgeous red hair, smooth skin and an hourglass figure, it's no surprise she has been locked down all this time; if anyone is announcing an engagement soon it will be her. She openly gives her opinion about anything, whether it will hurt your feelings or not.

Then there is Chloe who became a successful fashion designer aged 25, making her a young multimillionaire, not to mention being blessed with her naturally thin frame, possessing long shiny blonde hair which cascades past her waist and no need to wear makeup as she looks stunning 24/7. There are plenty of reasons to be jealous of her. Although her personality is no rich bitch — she doesn't flaunt her wealth like you would assume, she is 100% beautiful inside and out.

"So Freya, how was your hot teacher today?" Chloe questioned with a giggle as she poured a glass of wine for everyone.

"Oh my god, irritatingly hot," she spoke as she munched on some kettle crisps. "I would have been kicked out if I acted on my thoughts when I first touched his body during my assessment today." She paused, sipping her wine. "I'm so glad it's over, I couldn't get out of there fast enough, come to think of it I don't even think I said bye," she giggled.

"Oh my god, Freya you are awful," Nina spoke with embarrassment.

"Nina, Miss Pure of Heart, you do not want to know what was running through my mind. I had to start twice, although I am hoping I passed my assessment in the end." She crossed her fingers. "I just wish I could have him! He sends me crazy. I doubt he would ever feel the same, I am 99% sure he hates me, probably has a right opinion of me. I'm always late and distracted, he will be glad to see the back of me this summer," she continued.

"Don't worry, tomorrow night we will get you what you need and you can forget about him. Well, until next week," Louise responded.

"Seriously Freya, get a boyfriend, then you can have sex whenever you want," Nina nagged.

"Oh don't worry, I have sex whenever I want, with whoever I want," Freya blurted out.

"Ye but these flings mean nothing, don't you want something more? First there was Jack and now there is Matt, both guys you can't have," she reminded her.

"Ouch, Nina. Ouch. One day maybe, but I like having fun at the moment," Freya said whilst glancing at Louise with a cheeky smile, trying not to let her comment get beneath her skin.

"Right, who are we, Team Mark Darcy, or team Jack?" Chloe butted in, placing Bridget Jones' Baby into the DVD player. "God, I am Daniel Cleaver all the way," she laughed.

Saturday came by so fast, with work having been so busy. During her afternoon shift she had finished late, ruining her plans of going shopping for a new outfit for her leaving party. She had worked in a busy upcoming bar in her local town for the past four years. Each day was the same, the same regular faces were seen and the same old conversations were spoken, however she did not seem to mind being in the lamp-lit, cosy, dark wooden dressed room for so long due to the skills and friends she had made along the way. Plus the benefit of being able to have extra money on top of her student loan and an amazing boss who let her work flexible shifts around her assignments. Although she did often repay the favour if she was free by offering to work overtime during busy seasons. Her dedication had promoted her to team leader for the past year which also helped her bank balance. Working late shifts and every weekend was a breeze though she was glad to be hanging up her apron and having the summer off before she looked for a full-time job.

*

With a big night out occurring in few hours she has no choice other than to wear an old outfit found in the back of her wardrobe. Her long brown hair, fierce dark brown eyes and dark red lips are complemented by a tight black spaghetti-strapped dress cut above her knees. Often wearing Converse, the only other option is black suede ankle boots which positively agree with her attire. Typically it is raining outside, meaning her straight hair will most likely kink and her makeup will run. Luckily being no girly girl or makeup artist, her simple eyeliner skills still manage to make her eyes stand out from her freckled face, enough to make anyone stop and stare.

Arriving late for her own leaving party, she emerged into the bustling bar where she finished her last shift earlier this afternoon, now full of people, girl groups, couples and work friends all enjoying the busy Saturday night atmosphere. Hardly able to hear over the noise of conversations and loud music being played, she walked around looking upon the friendly faces she had come to know. The wooden bar covered in freshly pulled pints, juicy cocktails in frosted glasses dressed with fresh fruit and evening snacks made her crave a tasty drink and her stomach rumble, now regretting the choice of not eating before coming out.

"Finally. Where have you been?" she heard. Louise grabbed her bag, placing it on the bar and replaced it with a raspberry cocktail, one of her favourites. Taking a large sip through the straw the fruity flavours refreshed her along with a bite of the strawberry garnish. Leaning over the bar to her recent colleague she waved, ordering a small pot of mixed nuts to fill her hunger for a while.

"You have some catching up to do, girl, get drinking," Louise sniggered, sounding tipsy.

She enjoyed circling her colleagues, the bar regulars and friends; it seemed everyone she had invited had turned up to wish her good luck for the future. A beautiful girl like her was often flirted with and blushing at compliments although she had become known for always turning down gents' offers to date due to a busy student lifestyle and the preference of one-night stands after a boozy night out. Now her assessments were over she had decided for tonight she was on the prowl in desperate need to satisfy the hunger within her body caused by Matt just yesterday.

"Anyone catching your eye?" Louise laughed as she noticed Freya eyeing up the room. "I know what you're thinking."

"Ha-ha," she chuckled. "Oh I don't know, Louise, what's happened to me? Nina's right, I have the past of being broken-hearted and now I've turned into a one-night stand. Don't get me wrong, I enjoy the sex but I'm still alone every morning. Why is it that everyone I want I can't have?" she questioned as she sipped another cocktail dry.

"Argh, Freya, don't kill the mood! Don't worry, tonight you can let loose! No more course work! Just relax and let the night take you away. Plus, you're looking that hot I am even tempted to come home with you," laughed Louise.

"Oi," Freya chuckled, nudging her. "Anyway, I best go and mingle and say my farewells," she said as she walked away from the bar.

"You will be missed," a deep tone spoke from behind her, making her turn.

"Hi Bradley." She playfully smiled, biting her straw. Bradley, who she had noticed become more of a regular as time went on, was stood before her. She observed him; he was in great shape. Having a hands-on job seemed to keep him fit. Being three years her junior she considered him as a friend; they always managed to have a laugh plus the constant flirting they tossed back and forward every shift made her enjoy his company. He would generally stand on the other side of the bar, always wearing his loose work clothes or jeans and shirts which in all these years had never allowed anything to be given away as to what kind of body was to be found under his clothes. Although she seemed to entertain his personality and she enjoyed the teasing, nothing had ever happened between them, but she was sure he had always been curious. He looked good tonight, his blond hair waxed into a quiff, his eyes sparkling as she looked into them. He smelt amazing as usual as she stood secretly inhaling his scent.

"I do have to say you look gorgeous, considering you could get away with working tonight. Black clothes as always?" he expressed, obviously looking her up and down.

"Ha, well I thought if they get busy I could jump behind the bar," she joked. "But thank you for the compliment, I think," she playfully grinned.

Having lost count of the number of drinks she had sipped dry, she felt tipsy and started swaying as she stood engrossed in conversation, her body tingling and feeling frisky. She couldn't help but stare into his dark blue eyes, imagining her fingers tugging on his long, rugged, blond hair whilst his hands firmly caressed her free breasts, not to mention her no underwear situation.

"Freya, are you alright?" Bradley was concerned.

"Yep, I'm good," she responded, questioning herself after a night of mingling with plenty of attractive men, why on earth she was having these thoughts about Bradley, whom until now she had never fancied hooking up with, seeing as she had never fancied anyone younger than her. She found a seat upon the sofa next to Louise and joined in with her conversation to steer herself away from something she might regret.

As the middle of the night crept in the bar had emptied and she was feeling worse for wear now the amount of alcohol she had consumed hit her without warning. She collected her things and expressed her goodbyes to her now ex-colleagues. Standing in the doorway keeping out of the rain, waiting for a taxi, she heard a familiar voice from over the garden fence. Having thought she was the last there she went to see who it was. Pulling open the garden door, Bradley sat there smoking his cigarette, talking on the phone, looking right at her. He hung up almost immediately.

"I thought you left ages ago?" she asked, stepping down the step, placing her bag on the bench beside her.

"Well yes, I was going but something kept me from leaving," he teased, lifting himself from under the bench, making his way slowly towards her with a look in his eyes, causing tension within her body. She moved herself backwards until she felt the wall's cold bricks against her bare skin, making her gasp. Bradley stood in front of her within reach, he placed his arms firmly against the wall either side of her so she could not escape his grasp. "I've had some naughty thoughts about you and they keep me up at night," he confessed with his breath warm, close to her, smelling of cigarette smoke and liquor, a scent she actually favoured to her surprise, sending her body into a frenzy. Staring into his eyes she felt on edge, she found herself biting her lip so hard the taste of blood filled her mouth. The tension sent sparks between them. As he lowered an arm to move away she thrusted a kiss upon his welcoming lips. As they fell into a passionate, tasty moment no words were spoken as he pulled her towards his body, placing her against the wall. Feeling shocked with herself but completely in awe of the moment she moved her hands to his hair, tugging at him, letting it become obvious what she wanted. Moving her hands up above her, he held them in position whilst nibbling her neck, removing her straps from her shoulders with his teeth.

The dress falls straight to the floor, leaving her completely naked other than her boots. Releasing her hands she unbuckles his belt, tugging at his jeans where she feels him, hard. He caresses her erect nipples with his tongue with his hand now between her legs. Warm and wet, he inserts two fingers, circling her g-spot.

Experiencing a feeling she had wanted to fill her body for some time, she groans for more, feeling too horny and drunk to care about anyone hearing. Her naked body pushes against him, now straddling him on the table of the bench. His large pulsing member ready and waiting beneath her.

It doesn't come as a surprise to her that he is excellent with his hands as he seems to know exactly where to put them to make her body tremble with arousal. Taking control, she places his hard cock in her mouth, tasting him, swirling her tongue around his penis, taking in as much as she can. She's hungry for him, his breathing quickens, bringing him closer to climax. He's not ready quite yet.

Guiding her up, he raises her onto his cock; as he enters her slowly she shudders. Huge and solid, he fills her. As her hips thrust back and forth friction between her knees and the wood make her wince. He lifts her up with her legs wrapped around him, placing her upon the table, pounding deep into her, making her body tense with every thrust. Close to orgasm he slows, stood fucking her as he takes in all her body as he looks on.

"You're incredible, just like I expected," he spoke, breaking the silence.

Eager to touch him she lifts her body, grabbing the back of his neck. He moves her closer towards him, and he's as deep as he can go. He thrusts harder and harder over and over again; she moans, his movements hard and deep bring her to climax whilst he explodes inside her.

"Fuuuck," was all she could process whilst coming back to reality. Sliding out of her juicy entrance he stands, redressing himself. Laying naked in all her glory, he passes her his hand, helping her up as she catches her breath. Arising looking full of sex, she slides her dress back on, covering her body, leaving him now looking disappointed.

Opening the garden door, making her way back to the exit little was said. Bradley behind her took her hand into his as he lit a cigarette with the other; she found this so sexy about him.

"Fancy round two back at mine?" he propositioned.

She looked at him questioning whether she should decline, although him standing there looking as hot as he did with now scruffy hair and smelling so good was hard to resist.

"Try and stop me," she smirked.

CHAPTER 3

Hungry for More

The weekend came and went as she spent most of the time romping with Bradley around his flat after leaving her party with him. With him being young and free it turned out he had no commitments at the weekend other than working in the bar. In her opinion he was definitely not boyfriend material for her but was amazing in bed and fun to play with. Enjoying the fact he was quite a talented guy when it comes to fore play and rough and tumbling she had lost count of how many times she'd climaxed this weekend, this being the only source of exercise which wasn't like her. As she made her walk of shame home in the dress she went out in two nights ago she grabbed her phone to type a message.

'Hi Chris. I'm sorry I cancelled, can I rearrange our first training session for tomorrow morning?'

He replied right back.

'Hi Freya, it's not a problem, 5am. See you there.'

*

After a good night's sleep she jumped out of bed

feeling alert and ready for her first session with her new personal trainer. A few months ago she applied for her first marathon on a whim, being a keen runner. When she received her magazine through the post she was shocked to have been accepted, dumbfounded, she felt she needed to commit to more training. Knowing Louise used a personal trainer she asked for his number to see if he had anything that may help her feel more reassured about her ability to complete the 26.2 miles in her goal of four hours.

Skipping out on breakfast she grabbed a bottle of fresh orange juice from the fridge for the drive over. Her mind reminiscing over her weekend antics with Bradley as well as dreading seeing Matt later on at university, she was amused with her recent behaviour. *So I have a man I keep fantasising about driving me mad and spent the whole weekend with a guy I can't shake off,* she thought, whilst discarding yet another text message from him asking to meet up again soon. Had Bradley now become her booty call? She smiled at the thought of having someone to release her sexual tension with.

After driving around a busy car park for what seemed like forever she finally managed to get parked and made her way to her usual gym where she spent most of her evenings when she was not running. Having being a member for four years she had never thought about having a personal trainer and when Louise mentioned it to her she was intrigued. During her workout sessions she often watched the trainers with their clients, most fitting the description of a bald, beefy 40-year-old man, someone she wouldn't like telling her what to do at 5am charging her £30 an hour. Hoping this was not the case she scanned her key card at the entrance and walked into the cold building as air-con blew down her back. As she scanned the room her freshly manicured nails tapped impatiently against her water bottle. The room was filled with familiar faces and was busier than she thought it would be this early in the morning; she could only assume everyone was out to get their beach bodies ready for the summer.

Over in the corner was the group of pretty, skinny, midriff-showing, sports bra-wearing girls who didn't need to be there but went purely for the male attention whilst making every other female feel intimidated. The usual buff lads surrounded the free weights – why she never used them, the studio was taken up with a spin class and several machines were occupied by the older generation. Why on earth they were up so early she did not know.

Sat over on the sofa against the wall behind the desk was a blond guy scrolling through his phone. She hadn't seen him before but from what she could see he had a huge upper body under a tight top with the most defined biceps and pecs she had ever seen, something she really fancied on a man. A warmth arose within her chest and between her legs; she felt a glow rise within her cheeks, now panicking that she looked like a beetroot in front of this godlike man. She sipped at her water in hope to cool down. His head lifted and he clocked her; he had the most handsome smile surrounded by neat but rugged facial hair, making her feel weak at the knees. He stood from the chair and walked toward her. *Oh no*, she thought to herself.

"Hi, I'm Chris, you must be Freya." He held out his hand towards her.

Holy shit, she thought as she shook it. His hands were large against hers, his touch sending electricity down her spine.

"Yes I am, sorry I am late, parking was mad," she nervously stuttered.

"No worries," he returned, checking her out in a noticeable way. "This way," he directed her, giving her a nod.

She looked up and down at the most stunning man she had ever seen. His body bulging through his clothes made her feel wet within her pussy; his biceps and triceps were pumped along with his huge broad shoulders; under his top she imagined solid pecs and a firm eight pack of abdominals.

"Follow me, we have a few forms to fill out first," he requested.

She followed him across the room eyeing up his fine-looking ass. His protruding thighs hidden under a pair of tight joggers looked like they were going to rip the seams when he walked. Struggling to find any words she realised she had been thrown into complete silence by the man she had just met; she felt completely intimidated. *Hurry up, Freya, say something clever,* she told herself.

"You're new here? Well not new-new? Look at your body, it's beautiful." She laughed, tongue tied.

Oh crap. Where did that come from? she thought, kicking herself.

"Ha, I don't work within this gym, I just use its

facilities for personal training," he smirked, trying not to laugh.

Chris was looking at her with his blue eyes; she wondered how much of a twat he already thought she was. Although she was pretty sure he was used to girls getting tongue tied over him, he must be sure of himself.

"So we have a few forms to fill in, you know, the usual health declarations etcetera, then I need to take your measurements, we will then make a workout schedule and then go from there, sound alright?" he asked.

She listened to every word that came out of his mouth as if it was coming out in slow motion. She hadn't noticed she was licking her lips until excess saliva started to bubble out of her mouth. *Oh God, what is wrong with my body this morning?* she exclaimed to herself as she nodded in agreement.

"Right, go in there, I'll grab my stuff and be with you in a second," Chris requested in his manly tone.

Still silent, she made her way to what she thought was going to be a room; as she opened the door it was just one of the bathrooms which held a shower. Questioning whether she had walked into the wrong room she turned to walk out. The handle went with Chris shutting the door behind him. The room was small, just enough space for the two of them, but pretty tight. Feeling awkward she tried her hardest not to giggle with embarrassment; she didn't know where to look, he was in arm's reach of her, making her feel flustered, her palms sweating. On the other hand he looked at complete ease. Chris passed her a clipboard with a sheet to fill in. As she took it she admired his big hands, noticing no wedding ring; she beamed. She filled in the form trying to sound as clever as she could using sports vocabulary which she had picked up from university. She felt his eyes burning into her whilst he waited.

"What do you do then, Freya?" he asked, trying to make small talk.

"I've nearly finished my last year of university studying sports science as well as working in a bar for four years but I've just quit so I can have the summer off. I had my last assignments last week so I'm hoping to get some feedback today, I'm actually quite nervous about it really," she went on, questioning herself as to why she elaborated so much.

"Interesting course. I never did university, but I have several sports and fitness qualifications," he responded with a smile.

She gawked up at him as she passed back the clipboard, her fingers touching his as she did. She wanted to ask so many questions and find out about him but held herself back.

"Let's do your height and weight," he asked. As for most girls, this would be their worst nightmare. Freya on the other hand was not worried about her weight, knowing she stood at five foot four, weighing in at nine stone. This was her current favourite size and she tried extremely hard to maintain it. Chris then pulled out an apparatus she recognised and her heart sank due to embarrassing memories.

"Can I do your body composition? It's much more accurate than BMI," he asked.

"OK," she responded nervously.

Chris brought his body closer to hers; within the room there wasn't any space to move, their bodies basically touching, not that she minded. Her cheeks flushed as he took hold of her small biceps, her legs tingling with arousal. As he requested to do her stomach area she lifted her top, exposing her tanned stomach with slightly visible lines where her abs were starting to poke through. She watched him as he concentrated and wished she had done a much more professional job at Matt's body composition now, worrying about her assessment grade. *If only I had this session last week,* she thought.

"Just your thighs left," he insisted. She felt relieved she chose to wear baggy shorts this morning rather than her usual tight leggings. Chris crouched down taking her smoothly shaved leg; for a moment it felt like he ran his warm hand up her leg making his way to her thigh, making her shiver.

She gasped, her heart started to pound within her chest, her loins filled with warmth and her sex filled with juices. She stared at him with a flushed look, imagining his sexy toned body beneath his clothes, craving to touch him. Visualising him taking hold of her right now up against the wall was making her smirk.

"We're done, let's get going," he ordered, looking at her with a confused frown. Could he see what she was thinking from her body language? She questioned herself as she snapped out of her daze.

She took a deep breath as she walked into the much cooler gym space, shaking her head discreetly, trying to overcome these naughty images. Chris took her into the now free studio; he grabbed a 10kg kettle bell and asked her to perform squats and lunges. Something she rarely did.

Oh great, she thought, *he's going to have a right gawk at my ass performing incorrect squats when I'm supposed to be good at this. Why on earth I told him I studied sports I don't know!*

She stood with her legs shoulder width apart and bent down into a squat, grabbing the kettle bell on her way up. She repeated this. She felt unsure of herself as he watched. He ordered her to perform a few more causing her to break a sweat; her legs started to shake.

"Right, stop there, you have the right technique although you need to push your bum further back and your thighs more forward when returning to standing," he described. "Watch me."

He took hold of a 20kg kettlebell and stood in front of her. He bent down and pushed his buttocks right back, displaying one finely pert rear end; as he rose he pushed his thighs hard forward which faintly showed his bulge hidden beneath his layers.

"Got it?" he queried.

She nodded with a smirk and started again, pushing her ass out as far as she could when bending. She looked up, embarrassed. "Like this?" she laughed.

"That's it," he grinned as he checked her ass out. Freya was sure she noticed a slight flushed look now within her trainer's face. She wondered if he felt as horny as she did.

Following a gruelling hour of leg and butt sets and firm rolling ordered by Chris, he finally told her she was free to go. "I can see what we need to work on to get you fitter for this marathon and it's doable as long as we have one-on-one sessions often," he told her as they walked to his sports bag which he started to pack his stuff into. She handed him £30, glaring into his eyes, her own wandering down to his welcoming lips, self-conscious of how sweaty and red she was. She smiled. "I'm up for that, it was nice meeting you," she declared.

"You too, have a good day and say hi to Louise for me," he requested as he walked out of the building. She watched him walk to his car, a nice shiny black Audi parked right outside. He never looked at her again. She made her way back to her car, climbing into her old navy blue Ford Focus. She grabbed her phone from her glove box, searched for Louise's name within her contact book…

'*You Bitch!*' she texts.

'☺ *did you enjoy your breakfast? Hot isn't he! Hahahaha,*' she receives back.

On her drive home she tried to relax, now feeling like she would now be in a tizzy for the rest of the day. She shuffled through her disks with one hand on the steering wheel as she placed an old CD she was once made as a gift into the player. Remembering the old days cleared her mind of her embarrassing gym session. She favoured the old music and often wished she could relive the days which were not so taken over by technology. As her mind pondered over Matt, having not seen him at university for her last hand-in sessions she wondered if she would see him again as she hoped to look upon his beautiful face, into his dark green eyes, locking in every detail of his muscular body, his voice, his mannerisms and his beautiful scent. She needed to remember everything about him, she wanted to. She had her fingers crossed to bump into him at graduation. Arriving home, she soon forgot about the beating her legs had just endured as she soon came face to face with the ground. Her legs failed to work beneath her as she climbed out of the car, her muscles feeling like jelly. She made her way back to her feet, picking up her phone and water bottle, looking around, making sure she hadn't been seen making a fool of herself as she dusted the gravel off her bare legs. *What a dick,* she thought. She sniggered. "My legs are going to hurt tomorrow," she said to herself, walking to her front door.

The weather was glorious and warm, just how she liked it, but before she wasted her summer days just sitting in the garden under the hot sun, with her head in a book, she decided to occupy herself by decorating her dated house.

She had managed to buy her own house having saved most her wages plus a little help from her mum and dad as well as living off her student loan. Her pretty-looking detached house was placed in the countryside just outside the main town where the nearest shop was found. One street of houses with a small playground for the few small children living a few doors down was surrounded by nothing but empty fields, the quiet surroundings she had come to love with the benefit of running routes. Her home consisted of three bedrooms, a large open kitchen-diner entailing immaculate light blue units complementing white cupboards and a huge light oak table for when her family and friends ever visited. Her lounge was warm and homey with an open lit fireplace for the cold evenings and defined by a light brown carpet and green walls; this was the first to be changed. She had decided on an off-beige colour with one feature wall which surrounded the fireplace. Her favourite house feature was her staircase, this was long and opened up, parting into two landings, one with a spacious bathroom and a large spare bedroom, on the opposite landing the big main bedroom and ensuite and another smaller bedroom which she was currently using as her office to do her assignments in, plus an exercise bike which was now draped in coats and bags. Looking out from her bedroom she had a lovely driveway which consisted of a large drive bordered by a two-way open brick wall and garden bushes which she preferred as she disliked looking after flowers. To the back of the house decking was seen upon which her unused BBQ sat and hot tub which her friends were very fond of. Stepping off the decking was a large lawn big enough for a dog to run around if she ever decided to have one. Currently her house was too big just for her but it was the way she liked it.

She danced away to the latest dance tunes playing through the radio, dressed in scruffy denim short dungarees hiding a body-hugging vest top, completely covered in paint which she had also managed to brush through her scruffy up hairdo. She felt a sudden thirst and hunger after realising it was 4pm and she hadn't eaten all day after starting at 9 that morning. Being Thursday night, her friends otherwise occupied she decided to go and grab a bottle of rosé, a takeout meal from her favourite Italian restaurant and her favourite box of chocolates to sit and eat in front of a chick flick after a hard day's work. She grabbed her keys and clambered into her car and drove into the town ten minutes away. The atmosphere along the streets were busier than expected, teenagers were seen strolling the streets in groups, busy mums were rushing around dragging their toddlers by their arms as they bought last-minute holiday clothes for the upcoming summer holidays before the shops became busy over the weekend. Businessmen on the phone walked in between cars without an ounce of respect for the traffic and couples out walking hand-in-hand for evening meals and drinks. It was an upcoming fact Thursday had now become the new Friday.

After collecting her parking ticket she made her way to the Italian and ordered her dinner; whilst waiting she walked to the nearest Tesco down the street. As she felt the warmth of the sunshine on her skin she decided her plan for tomorrow was to sunbathe due to the predicted temperatures of 32 degrees. As she walked into the cool supermarket she grabbed a bag of white chocolate buttons, milk buttons and chocolate-covered raisins.

"Still your favourite then?" she heard from over her shoulder. She recognised the voice and turned around, pleading that it was the person she thought it was.

"JACK!" she squealed. "What are you doing here?" As she hugged him tightly, he returned the gesture.

"I thought you were away! I haven't seen you in ages, I was going to text you the other day after I found some photos of you," she continued, not letting him getting a word in edgeways.

He smiled and laughed. "Geeze, calm down. Ye, I'm back for summer leave."

"Literally just finished?" she questioned as she observed his current outfit.

Jack stood opposite her covered in her favourite colour, khaki green, looking ridiculously fine in his army uniform which he had acquired at 16 years old. They were high school sweethearts; they met when they were 14 years old and having grown into their mid-teens together they felt like they were in love. They experienced their first sexual experiences with each other as they became legal and built a bond so strong they became inseparable until the day he broke the news to her that he was going to army foundation in the September following his 16th birthday. She left, heartbroken at the feeling of being without him, which she had to learn to overcome as distance and time tore them apart. They contacted each other every day with a phone call each night in the beginning; they soon started writing letters to each to each other each week and spent time together every time he came home. But it had been years; she one day decided she couldn't handle saying goodbye anymore and called it a day. Even though it destroyed her it allowed him to achieve within his career and her to grow up without him.

Having grown up together she had watched him grow from a skinny boy into a good-looking charming lad, into the masculine soldier he was today. His hair, shaved due to his career was a shade of dark brown with a hint of glistening grey, his eyes as blue as a summer's sky and his sun-kissed face clean shaven. His body, big and muscular from carrying heavy loads looked to be showing no signs of weakness. She wished they hadn't grown apart and wondered what his life was like.

"I see you're decorating?" he asked, looking down at the state she was in. She now slightly wished she had washed and changed as she blushed.

"Ye, I decided to decorate my house. It was feeling a little dated so I thought I would have a go before spending the summer in the garden after graduation," she explained.

"Sounds nice, assuming a good-looking girl like you has a boyfriend helping you out?" He immediately questioned her love life.

She beamed as he seemed as interested in her life as he always had been, she would say kind of protective in the hope she would never move on from him.

"Err no, just me, single, and no boyfriend, in my big house enjoying life," she returned to his delight.

His eyes were looking right into hers, which made her feel intimidated; she did not want to tell him he was the last boyfriend she'd actually had and in the past nine years she had just been having fun. She was pretty sure his story was different and that he was coming home to visit his mum having most likely left a wife and kids somewhere near his army barracks. He was the kind of guy to settle down quickly.

As she glanced at her watch he noticed; he grabbed some Boost bars and sweet packets. "Sorry I've kept you."

"No, no you haven't I've just popped in her whilst my dinner cooks, I need to go and collect it. I would love to catch up when you're free." Subtlety inviting him over.

"Well I have nowhere to be if you want some company?" he asked with a smile.

"What, now? Of course, come back to mine with me then," hiding her excitement.

Freya grabbed a bottle of fruity rosé and bottle of lemonade whilst she passed the drinks aisle as they made their ways to the tills. They threw back small-talk as they collected her dinner which he offered to pay for, although she declined and he followed her in his car back to her house.

Making their way through her front door, hands full with dinner, drinks and snacks, they were having a laugh about the good old days that they had spent together and all the silly things they used to do. She felt more than relaxed around Jack, like they had never been apart. He felt the same, but knowing he was leaving again stopped her from getting too comfortable. She walked him into the kitchen where she plated up their dinner, halving hers with him, and prepared some drinks. Jack stuck to lemonade as alcohol was not his thing, something she admired about him and always had. They sat among the large oak kitchen table for hours talking about their lives; she told him about her university course, her previous job, and her friends – he knew only of Louise. He expanded on what time abroad was like, his army mates and the stories he had, all of which she could not imagine but found fascinating.

It was nearing 10pm; the light had faded from the garden which was shining bright when they first sat down. She had drunk a whole bottle of wine to her surprise and munched her way through most of her snacks, her belly now feeling bloated. He was sprawled out before her on his chair with his legs out straight, arms crossed, sat in his army trousers and a dark green t-shirt. She loved his look and was adamant he was the only one who could pull it off so well. Feeling happy, tipsy and horny, she was trying to pass off she was up for some fun as she stroked his tattooed arm, flirting, making him smile. She did not want to ask or make a pass without looking stupid if he was to decline her, something she was not used to.

"Do you want a house tour, seen as we have sat here all night?" she wondered.

"Ye, go on then, let's see how bad your painting really is," he joked, standing up straight into his natural army stance. He followed her in to the hallway as they explored around downstairs.

"My favourite thing in this house is the stairs," she beamed as they made their way.

"I remember you saying you wanted this kind of layout when we were young. It seems you have worked hard to get here, Freya, you should be proud of yourself." He paused. "I can't say the same for me, living in an army barracks with other lads and coming home to the same bedroom you saw nine years ago at my mum's house," he commented with a disheartened tone.

"I highly disagree, you have worked on a career, something I yet have to do," she reassured him.

Jack took in every detail of the house as he wandered around; he was keen to learn what kind of woman Freya had become just by seeing her chosen surroundings.

"Finally this is my bedroom, and the en-suite is through there." She pointed her hand towards to the bathroom whilst she observed Jack peering around.

"So what do you think? Nice, huh?" she questioned, feeling proud, trying not to sound smug.

"It's a nice home, quite big for just one person," he laughed. "Your DIY skills aren't too bad either despite most of the paint being on yourself." He looked her up and down and brushed his hand over her paint-covered hair. Catching his eye as he lowered his arm, his hand fell onto her cheek, rubbing his thumb across her wet, plump, rose red lips.

"I could imagine you want to shower soon?" he questioned with a seductive tone. She stood unable to move, now he was sending signals and she felt frozen. *Will this ruin our friendship or shall I just have some fun whilst he's here?* she thought to herself.

Jack unbuckled her dungaree straps which fell to the ground, her curves on show through her tight vest and white lacy thong. He looked down at her as she looked up at him. She wobbled slightly due to the wine and the tingling running all through her body. *Screw it!* she told herself.

Taking her hands behind his soft, strong neck, caressing his big defined shoulders, she passionately placed a kiss upon his lips, nibbling at them as she released, their bodies touching. He responded with a huge bulge pulsing through his tightly worn trousers.

He nodded towards the bathroom.

"In there." He nodded his head towards the bathroom. She liked that idea, raising an eyebrow and a smile. Jack pulled her hair loose from its up-do; her locks fell upon her shoulders, sweeping over his face. Moving it aside gently with his long fingers, she flinched at the touch of him. She pulled at his top, he raised it over his head, throwing it aside. He lifted her top and unclipped her bra letting her breasts fall free, tanned and full, her nipples erect for him to take into his mouth if he wished. Kissing his neck, her hands slid all over his body whilst he undid his belt, letting his trousers fall to the floor. As they fondled each other she stood there in nothing but her lace thong, his face glowing.

His large erect penis looks unable to move under his soft boxers. Placing her hand below his waist she squeezes his ass, removing his last item of clothing. Her cold hand makes its way around to his welcoming cock; he stops her, grabbing her by the hand, directing her into the bathroom. She flicks on the shower and they climb in under the warm running water. Paint washing away from her hair and skin, touching his skin as it falls with the water.

She runs her hand through his thick hair. "Fuck me," she demands.

He kisses her forehead, making his way to her neck. He nibbles her ear, whispering, "Not yet."

She's waiting in anticipation, horny as ever, wanting his large cock to fill her pulsing pussy. Digging her nails into his back as he bites her soaked tit, moving from one to the other, his tongue playing with her nipples makes her quiver. He places kisses on her stomach as he makes his way to his knees. Nibbling the inside of her thigh, she shudders, entwining his hair into her fingers. Her breathing becomes heavy, she's looking up into the falling water with her eyes closed, taking it all in. His tongue now opening her lips, him tasting her juices for the first time. Cupping her peachy ass into his hands, he's taking her all in, thrashing his tongue against her clit. She's close to climax; her toes curl as she stands upon them trying not to fall, using the wall to lean on, allowing him further into her.

A powerful surge trembles through her body, her pussy now feeling numb but pulsing at the same time. Pulling him up from his knees his face hits the water, his cheeks reddened.

Horny for more she pushes him against the cold tiles, kissing him, pulling at his lips with her teeth. Her hand wraps about his erect dick, stroking it back and forth as he moans. Enjoying her touch, he is ready to fuck her. Spinning her round to face the wall, holding her waist, his large cock enters her from behind. She groans, he's deep within her, so large and naturally ribbed. He thrusts, each one making her gasp. Water cascades down her body, her hands leaning on the wall giving her balance as she's bent over. His hands caress her body, pulling on her long, soaked hair. He pounds quicker, his breathing rate increasing. His strong legs allowing him to work harder, his dick, hard, really hard. Moving his hands to her hanging breasts. She moans.

"Give it to me harder!" she screams.

"Oh my god," he lets out as he takes a deep breath,

releasing his orgasm. He holds her waist tightly, guiding her to stand. She turns, looking deep into his eyes and smiles. Placing a kiss upon her lips, he stands beneath the falling water.

"I like the bathroom," he says as he climbs out, making his way into the bedroom. She stays and washes her hair quickly; as she wraps a towel around her she sees Jack is already dressed.

"I have to get going," he tells her as she looks up at him, holding off asking why, feeling completely used as she became silent with shock. She found herself nodding in agreement.

"Oh, OK." After such a great afternoon and mind-blowing sex she feels disappointed he's quickly running out on her; it takes everything within her to avoid confrontation. He walks towards her and kisses her on the cheek.

"Thanks for a great catch-up, sorry I've got to rush off," he said as he made his way down the stairs. She watched him shut the front door behind him.

Stood in nothing but a towel she walks to the window to watch him walk to his shiny blue BMW. As he opened the door he looks up at her, giving her a wave with a look in his eyes she had seen before. He turns on his ignition and lights and drove out of her driveway. He was not just arriving back for summer, he was leaving.

CHAPTER 4

Graduation

Friday morning soon drew round, after Jack's sudden departure from their evening together. She dressed herself in baggy pyjamas which she spent the day watching a series on Netflix in. Feeling lonely since seeing so many people the past weekend, she took to bed early in hope that the harrowing feelings she felt would be gone by the time she woke up. Opening her eyes, she squinted to adjust to the sunlight which was beaming into her bedroom; the smell of fresh paint stung her nose as she felt she was going to be nursing a migraine for the day, most probably caused by the wine and chocolate she consumed the night before. Glancing a look to her clock she saw it was already 10am and she really had slept in. She laid wrapped within her duvet; she grabbed her phone from her bedside unit, no messages. For some reason she was expecting one from her most recent lover. Her tummy was churning.

Scrolling through her phone she group messaged her girls' group.

'Can we grab coffee… need a chat… did something stupid.'

'I'm free,' replied Nina.

'Starbucks in 20,' texted Louise.

'See you there,' Chloe wrote.

She felt lucky to have such an amazing group of friends who would be there pretty much whenever she needed. She jumped out of bed, brushed her hair, tying it into a high ponytail, splashed some water on her face and added some lip balm onto her chapped lips. She grabbed a plum skater dress and black leggings, completing her outfit with some white Converse. Grabbing her keys, she locked the door and left to meet her friends.

Starbucks was busy as she scanned the room – it was full of business meetings, mums' groups and workers rushing around with trays full of orders. She clocked her friends in the corner already sipping their drinks with one for her alongside a slice of fruit toast and a blueberry muffin. She smiled. This was not a one-off occurrence, her friends expected her to be curing a hangover along with a story about some lad she had hooked up with. She pulled out her chair and sat down.

"Morning, thanks for being free for me," she murmured.

"I needed the break anyway," Chloe insisted. "Come on then, which one is it this time? Please tell me it's the lecturer," she quizzed with a giggle.

"I'll get straight to it. It was stupid, I don't know why I did it, I feel stupid." She paused. "I slept with Jack," she admitted with disgrace, looking at each of her friends as they processed the information.

Louise being the only one to have met Jack, quickly fired back her opinion. "What the hell! Where did this come from?" with an irritated tone. "Don't go back there, you'll just get hurt." She threw a glance towards Nina, hoping for the same reaction.

"Freya, what are you doing? You already have too many options in my opinion, not to mention adding another one," Nina frowned, trying not to sound judgemental.

"Girls, less of the negativity, let's hear the story first," Chloe requested, shooting an intrigued look at Freya.

Her foot tapped against the leg of the chair as her fingers unconsciously drummed against her now empty coffee mug. She went on to speak undisturbed for 15 minutes.

After processing all the information regarding Freya's love life, opinions from Louise, Nina and Chloe were thrown in, making the situation more confusing. Of course Nina thought she should work on a relationship with Jack as it seemed some unwanted feelings arose when he was present.

"I don't want a relationship, Nina, I've told you before, when I knew he was leaving for a career in the army our chance of being together was over, I don't do long distance. I could love him, but I don't, these are childhood memories that spring my stomach into butterflies, not current feelings. Plus, I haven't even heard from him since we fucked, what does that say about his feelings towards me? He upped and left," she emphasised as she became infuriated about the way he treated her.

"I think you should make yourself look irritable this afternoon for your graduation and just hit on Mr Jones," Chloe expressed with a giggle.

"Holy shit, I forgot about that, I need to go and find something to wear. Anyone free for a shop?" Freya questioned, changing the conversation she had now grown tired of.

"Sorry, I have bits to do, I'll see you there though," Nina apologised.

"I have a workout with Chris, sorry," Louise said, throwing a smirk towards Freya.

"Have fun, I'll see you later, 4pm, don't be late," Freya spoke with a jealous tone towards Louise.

Freya stood tall from her seat, as did Chloe. "I'm free for a quick look around, I'll help you look sassy," she laughed.

Crossing the road, Chloe and Freya headed towards the clothes shops, not the biggest selection was found in a small town. Freya often preferred the usual John Lewis and Selfridges in comparison to the smaller chains but with the help of Chloe's expertise she was sure to find something rather than throwing something on from her wardrobe. You only graduate once, right? She planned to go the extra mile to look as nice as she could, knowing it was the last time she would see Mr Jones. Shifting through the clothes rails, it all seemed to be crop tops, denim shorts and thin-strapped dressed due to the current summer season.

"I'm going to find nothing at this rate, unless I want to look like I have just left the beach. I've left it too late," she huffed as she glanced through the items hanging.

"How about this?" she heard coming from the rack opposite. Due to Chloe's fashion background she often had the eye for items hidden away at the back of a rack. Freya often trusted her judgement.

Chloe walked over to Freya holding a lilac dress; it was a simple low-cut dress, sure to be tight to the skin, displaying her slim figure and allowing her pert bust to draw the eye. She was happy to purchase the dress without even trying it on. On the way to the till she grabbed some beige strapped high-heeled shoes to complement her dress. Thankful for her help, she thanked Chloe and gave her a ride home which consisted of girly music and a chin wag about their outfits and hairstyle ideas for their evening event.

After a morning of girl talk and retail therapy, she had now forgotten about Jack and had her mind completely set on trying to flatter Mr Jones. With only a few hours to go until her graduation party she soaked in a hot bubble bath surrounded by a nice-smelling candle, sipping on a glass of rosé wine. She became lost in thoughts about the past three years of Matt being her eye candy; as her mind wandered onto Matt's sexy body she started to feel a warmth in-between her thighs. Feeling horny, Freya sipped the last sip of her wine and lowered her hand between her legs, rubbing her clitoris, arousing her even more.

With the hot water flowing over her body, steam within the air and her heart beating fast she becomes flushed. Lifting one foot out of the water, placing it on the cold tap in hope to cool her slightly, her fingers gently circulate around her sensitive area whilst her other hand caresses her breast.

Her mind locked on her wild image of him

nibbling upon her neck, their legs entwined with his fingers wrapped within her long brown hair. Pumping hard into her wet pussy, him deeply breathing on her naked skin. Her eyes gazing into the tense look which he always places upon her. "Fuck me," she whispers. Her fingers now lashing against her clit hard and fast, she's close to climax, arching her back, lifting herself above the water, she takes a deep breath as her body tenses sending shivers down her spine, her toes curling. Opening her eyes she smiles, relaxing back into the bath, letting out a deep breath. Looking around at her surroundings she breathes in the smell of the burning candle and pours herself another glass of wine. After half an hour collecting her thoughts she is now to get ready for her graduation, in hope she doesn't blush upon the sight of Mr Jones.

She flicks through her iTunes selecting a pre-made playlist which she uses every time she gets ready for a party. Her phone vibrates in her hand.

'Fancy a drink tonight?! It's been a while ☺' she reads from Bradley. Oh, it has been a while since their last get-together, she smirked.

'I can't tonight it's my graduation tonight, RAIN CHECK,' she quickly typed back.

'Gotcha, another time,' he replied.

The thing Freya most liked about Bradley was his age showed through his actions; he would text for a cheeky weekend hook-up, no strings attached. As she stood texting Bradley she now saw where Nina was coming from when she said she had too many options – texting Bradley, masturbating over Matt and sleeping with Jack, not to mention these occurrences all being in the past 24 hours. *Oh my god, I've become a serial slut,* she thought as she stood looking at her reflection in the mirror. She shrugged her shoulders, smiled and continued to get ready, unfazed about the situation.

*

Her favourite upbeat songs blast through her bedroom walls whilst she stands wrapped within her large maroon towel. Realising she has nearly drunk a full bottle of wine already and it being mid-afternoon, she sensibly decides to switch to water and snacks on some crisps, relieved she's arranged a pick-up. Taking a seat at her dressing table she glances into the mirror, brushing the knots out of her wet hair as it drapes over her shoulders, soon enjoying the warm air upon her skin as she blow dries her hair. Twenty minutes pass; after choosing to straighten her hair and go for a natural make-up look she is left to cover her naked body. Making her way to her underwear drawer she selects a small laced thong which will be unnoticeable beneath her tight dress. As she tries her dress on for the first time she's relieved it fits perfectly; she tries it with a bra and without, getting her flustered as time is pressing. She stops faffing, deciding to dismiss the bra, feeling lucky to have such pert tits.

Her doorbell rings. Peering out of the window she sees Chloe waiting by her car, dressed in a hot pink dress, looking hot as usual. Bending down towards her mirror she adds shiny lip gloss onto her red rose lips, grabs her clutch bag and shoes and makes her way downstairs. Stumbling out the front door with her hands already full, she grabs her denim jacket and makes her way to the car.

"Looking fit!" Chloe shouts with a giggle.

"Thanks my lovely, you too." She laughs out loud.

Climbing into the car Freya places her shoes on her feet, buckling up the straps, and suddenly feels butterflies within her stomach.

Forty-five minutes pass as they hit little traffic as they laugh and sing along to 90s girl bands. Pulling up in the car park, the venue is busy, students are stood with their friends and family looking smart.

As Freya checks in she collects her graduation gown and cap which she drapes over her dress for the time being. The silk gown covers her skin, touching cool against her skin under the sun above. Peering around, the seats start to fill. Chloe, Louise, Nina and her boyfriend Ben are in their seats, her parents who could not make it due to them travelling the world in their much-deserved retirement had phoned her earlier that day and wished her congratulations and good luck.

"I'm so nervous," Freya announces, twiddling her fingers, staring up at the large stage she knows she will have to walk to in her high heels. "I hope I don't fall flat on my face up the steps," she laughs.

"You will be great. Once you have collected your award you can relax." Nina leans over, placing her hand on Freya's knee, giving it a squeeze, positively reassuring her.

"Freya, Freya," Louise whispers, "is that your lecturer?!" shifting a look towards the stage. Freya and all the girls glance over.

"Oh God, ye it is," she announces, sinking into her seat. Her heart pounds beneath her chest. Feeling a sudden urge to check how she looks and the current situation of her flushed cheeks she stays seated, trying to relax as her knees start to shake.

"He is well fit," Chloe loudly expresses with a smirk on her face, grabbing her compact mirror out of her clutch bag, checking her own make-up now she's seen some eye candy, then passing it to Freya. She peers around the lecturers noticing all the sports department are young, good-looking men.

"This might be a better party than I expected," she giggled, nudging her elbow into Louise with a mischievous look.

Eyeing up Mr Jones, Freya realises this is the first time in three years she has seen him in trousers. Standing there preparing the microphone, his body covered in an expensive-looking navy suit with a white shirt tucked underneath with brown shoes complementing his outfit. A completely different look to the sports gear and trainers but not to her surprise he looks gorgeous, clean shaven and his hair flowing free in the summer breeze. He certainly scrubs up well.

A vibration comes from within her bag; she quickly opens it, being discreet, switching it onto mute. Her phone hasn't stopped all day with messages wishing her good luck or congratulations for her graduation and future endeavours. Her heart sinks as she reads her screen *JACK*. Having been distracted with her graduation, Jack hadn't crept into her mind since he left her house the other night. With anxieties filling her stomach she dismisses the message for later and puts in back into her clutch. *It will just be another graduation-related message anyway,* she thought.

A tap on the microphone is heard, quietening

everyone, gaining everyone's full attention.

"Thank you everyone, friends and family, for joining our graduating students of summer 2018. We hope you enjoy the day, there is plenty to drink, a BBQ ready to eat and lots of activities to participate in following the awards."

Mr Jones speaks through the microphone, looking nervous for a change.

"Let's begin."

An hour passes; the hot July sun is shining down on everyone. Looking round, a few faces are a shade of pink. Luckily Freya's cap is protecting her head and face from burning.

"Freya Bell," is heard in the crowd.

"Oh no!" she mutters. Her wine now having worn off, she arises from her seat and climbs her way through the people surrounding her. Slowly strutting in her heels, she makes her way up the steps hoping she doesn't faceplant the floor. Looking directly into Mr Jones' eyes she smiles as if no one else was there watching. She's feeling pretty glad her gown covers her skin-tight dress right now as she's stood with everyone gawking at her. Their eyes lock as she collects her award from his hand, shaking it with the other one.

"Congratulations, Freya, well done." He smiles towards her.

"Thank you, sir," she grins. "Err, Matt! Sorry." She laughs nervously, he laughs back with a fiery look in his eyes.

She turns and walks back off stage towards her seat. Making her way safely to her chair, she lets out a deep sigh of relief, smiling at her friends. Watching on for the next half an hour as the graduation continues, each and every student looking nervous on their walk upstage with a sigh of relief as they walk off. Freya is now feeling parched; thinking about how downing a pint of water and sipping a nice fruity cocktail whilst eating a pulled pork roll from the BBQ would suffice right now, she misheard the graduation concluding.

"Let's go celebrate, graduate!" Her friends rise, grabbing her by the arm.

Leaving the rows of chairs Freya makes her way straight to the bathroom, redoing her face powder, lip gloss and combing her hair. Now all the photos have been done she is glad to be able to take off her gown, revealing her evening attire. One last glimpse into the mirror at her newly purchased lilac dress, she takes a deep breath and leaves the room.

Walking towards the bar to grab a drink she sees her friends have all perched upon a bench in the upcoming shade now the sun is going down. Each and every one of them already drinking and eating, she can't wait to full her rumbling belly with tasty food. She smiles to herself, proud of her achievements. She leans upon the bar waiting to be served, making small talk with the cute bar tender, her arse sticking out perfectly hugged by her skin-tight dress and her breasts leant upon her crossed arms on the bar as she watches her cocktail being made. Her long locks fall either side of her neck whilst she's feeling confident and relaxed for the evening. She feels a gentle touch to her waist. She turns to her oncomer expecting a friend; much to her surprise she observes Mr Jones standing closer to her than ever before.

As she turns towards him she nervously grins, he smiles back.

"Hi Freya, congratulations…" He seemed on edge for some reason, as he spoke.

"Thank you, Matt," she responded as she took her drink from the bartender, nodding her head his way as a thank you.

"After all this time you finally get my name right," he beamed. "I have something for you, you don't have to open it now, just make sure you do before next weekend," he requested as he handed her an envelope.

"Err, OK." She frowned with question. Eager to find out what it was she opened it there and then as Matt stood next to her; he ordered a beer at the bar as he looked on.

Opening the envelope inscribed with the university's logo, she pulled out what looked like an invitation. Printed on the institute's colours outlined in gold she read:

"In Honour of Outstanding Academic Achievement we are pleased to award **Freya Bell** *with the Excellence Award."*

Please attend our award ceremony on Saturday 20th July 7pm

Smart dress required.

Mr M Jones

As Freya skim read the remainder of the invite, she laughed, looking up at Matt. His eyes stared at her as if she was stood naked in front of him, she felt baffled.

"I don't understand," she quizzed.

"What is there not to understand? I put forward my recommendations within the sports department and everyone else agreed. You achieved the highest grade this year and have earned it through all the hard work you have put in," Matt explained in a friendly manner, taking a sip of his beer. As he looked on he admired the way she looked tonight in a subtle way.

"You disagree?" He stuttered as she fell silent, quickly sipping her cocktail dry, biting at her straw as she glanced towards him.

"In all honesty I thought you hated having me," she admitted.

Matts expression quickly changed, he looked confused. "No?! Why would you think that? Freya you have by far been one of my favourite students. You have made it easier for me to show up to work every morning for the past three years especially when you show up at your graduation dressed like that," he cheekily smirked.

She stepped back, grabbing her next drink from the bar, looking around as if to check she wasn't daydreaming. This current conversation was what she had been wanting to happen for the past three years, but now it was happening she was completely thrown her back. *Is he pissed?* crossed her mind. Not knowing what to think she felt a sudden urge to head back to her friends as she realised she had yet to make her way there, having been stood at the bar for nearly an hour and was now ravenous, although she had suddenly lost her appetite.

"Thank you, I guess, I'll take that as a compliment."

She looked back at her invitation.

"Something wrong?" he asked, looking at her body language, not seeming as enthusiastic as he expected.

"If I'm honest, you haven't been the nicest towards me, you were always snappy and distant," she jabbed. "I'm just going to go," she fired towards him as he stood silent with surprise. Taking her bag, drink and envelope she made her way outside. "Thanks for this by the way!" she shouted back at him, holding up her invite as she walked outside with a swagger knowing he was watching her leave the room. He did just that as he sat drinking his beer.

"Freya! There you are!" came a loud screech from the bench. By the sounds of it everyone but her was enjoying the party. As she looked upon all the empty drink glasses, *Prosecco* bottles and a tower of shot glasses, it was plainly obvious they were all shitfaced.

"Well at least you lot are making the most of the free bar," she spoke.

"I'm just going to the ladies, I'll grab more drinks," Chloe slurred as she stood with a wobble. "Freya you need to relax, you look so tense," she remarked, holding onto her for balance.

"What's up, Freya, you seem pissed off?" Louise questioned as she twiddled Freya's long hair, her face close to hers, allowing her to smell the liquor within her breath. Louise was known for the lack of body space she gave after a few too many to drink; right now Freya was not in the mood for it.

"Nothing, I'm fine, I just need a drink," shunning the conversation. Feeling annoyed at her reaction to Matt coming onto her, for what could have been her only chance to get with him, she sat in silence sipping her drink.

"OK," Louise finished.

"Here we go!" Chloe bellowed as she passed along drinks to everyone. "Shots for you, Freya," passing her a tray of several shots.

Not bothering to ask what they were, she took the tray, placing it in front of her, moving each shot glass with her thumb and forefinger until they were stood in a line. Taking the first one she shot it back without question, moving quickly onto the second, then the third, then the fourth. She took a breath as the taste of the mixture of spirits she just inhaled filled her mouth, burning her throat.

"Pure vodka, Chloe! What the actual…?" she went on to say.

"Oh pipe down, it's your graduation party and honestly your mood is killing the vibe," Chloe shouted across the table, too drunk to care about her volume of voice.

Hours passed and the party atmosphere was bustling; the benches were covered in glasses, bottles, and empty food plates. A bonfire was lit, adding warmth to the cool air. The flames lit the darkness alongside the fairy lights which hung among the bushes and trees. The smell of bonfire smoke, BBQ, cigarettes and alcohol was within the air. It was nearing midnight, surrounding her were mainly young groups of students and their friends. No kids or parents were in sight, her bench seemed to only have Nina and Ben on, who were still sipping *Prosecco*, engaged in their own conversation. Freya having been sat in the same position was now feeling beyond the ability to control her body; trying to elegantly climb from under the bench in her short dress and high heels, she found it hard to focus. Holding on tightly, she stood to her feet. Her head spun from the amount of alcohol surging through her body.

"Back in the minute," she slurred back at her table as she walked off, not that they were listening. Wobbling her way to the bar she stopped as she heard a noise beside her. Peering round the corner she saw a man and women going for it up against the brick wall of the building, both of them caressing each other's bodies, tugging on one another's clothes and hair, giggling and groping each other. As she went to turn she noticed the dress worn by the woman.

"Chloe!!" she shouted, startling the couple. They turned their heads toward her, embarrassed they had an audience. "Matt! Chloe! What the fuck?" she bellowed. Her stomach churned, she heaved, turning towards the nearest bush she threw up, managing to avoid her shoes and hair.

"Freya are you OK?" Chloe asked, moving Matt aside, walking towards her whilst straightening out her dress. Matt stood silent, unsure of what to do. For the second time this evening he had upset Freya, making her like him less and less.

Standing up straight, Freya struck Chloe with a bitchy scowl, the atmosphere tense amongst them. "Don't talk to me," she shunned. She left Chloe, heading straight for the bar.

"Freya!" Chloe followed.

"No Chloe, I don't want to hear it, just leave me

alone, I am going home," she howled at her, holding back her tears.

"I'm sorry," Chloe apologised as she backed off, disappearing out of sight.

"Can I have some water and a taxi please!" she requested the bar tender.

"Right away," he responded.

She left the bar to collect her bag, staggered her way to the bench, passing Matt on her way.

"Freya, calm down," he slurred, stepping towards her. "What's your problem? You snapped at me earlier and now you're making a scene over nothing," he implied.

"Matt, just leave it," she sneered. He definitely doesn't feel like her lecturer anymore.

"I'm going, guys, thanks for coming, I hope you enjoyed your night," she mumbled at Nina, Ben and Louise, and made her way to the entrance where she could see a taxi waiting.

"Oh, OK, bye," Nina spoke without question.

"Freya, what's happened?" she heard Louise shouting behind her.

Without explanation, her feet were now bare as she paced quickly to the car park. She climbed into the taxi with a sigh of relief that the night was over. Leaning her head against the window trying to calm herself down, she managed to stop herself from being sick once more. She gave the taxi driver her address and said nothing else.

As the car came to a stop outside her home she

opened her eyes and climbed out of the taxi. After spending five minutes trying each key in the front door she finally made it inside, throwing her shoes and bag on the ground she made her way upstairs as she held onto the banister. Her drunk body clambered straight into bed fully clothed; her head spun as if she was on a merry-go-round, causing her to heave. She climbed back out of bed. Picking up her glass from the bedside table she made her way into her bathroom. As she let the cold water run she took two paracetamols from her bathroom cabinet and shot them back, followed by a whole glass of water. She splashed her face several times in order to cool herself down and patted it dry, leaving her towel now covered in makeup. Making her way back to bed she pulled her duvet up over herself; she avoided laying on her empty stomach, having not eaten. Five minutes passed, she was now asleep.

CHAPTER 5

Booty Call

The sun beamed through her bedroom window where the curtains were still open from the day before. Sprawled out on her back, she lay squinting her eyes as they adjusted to the light. Holding her head, she knew she was in for a rough day. All she could taste was alcohol; the smell of smoke, sick and spirits lingered within her room and amongst her hair. Taking a glimpse at her clock she noticed it was 11:42am. *Oh my god, I've slept all morning,* she thought.

She sat up noticing her dress, tight, twisted and ridden up, she took it off over her head and threw it on the floor. Turning to the edge of the bed, now sat in nothing but her thong, she placed her feet on the soft carpet, holding onto the mattress whilst her stomach churned. Still feeling pissed, she slowly stood, making her way to her bathroom, climbing into the shower. The cold water hit her skin causing her to gasp; she slowly rinsed every scent of her evening away. After fifteen minutes of standing under the water she now felt fresh. Draping herself in a towel she went downstairs, picking up her bag on the way to the kitchen. She placed the envelope on the unit as she made her way to her phone. Looking at her phone she noticed…

Chloe 4 Missed Calls

Nina Text Message

Louise 2 Text Messages

2 Unread Emails

As she dismissed her missed calls from Chloe a feeling of anger and jealously surged through her as the image of her and Matt kissing replayed itself within her mind, their hands groping each other's intimate areas… *Urgh.* She shook her head. She was not yet feeling ready to talk to her about it although she knew it would have only been a drunken kiss, but still it was Matt. She continued to scroll through her texts from Nina and Louise whilst she stirred her tea.

Nina

Freya, let me know your home safely.

Talk to Chloe she feels awful.

Louise

Did you get home safe?? Chloe filled me in, I seemed to have missed everything.

Ring me!! Off to the gym although I feel shit!

Chris keeps asking me when you're next booking in.

Message him.

Lots of love

Her mind crossed to the thought of Chris' bulging biceps and dark blue eyes. Knowing her marathon was creeping up, Louise was right, she needed to get a training plan in place and back out running. *I'll ring him later,* she told herself.

Morning girls, or shall I say afternoon.

I'm home safe although I'm not feeling very healthy this morning. I went straight to bed and not long been up. Please don't let me drink again!

Chloe I'm sorry about my behaviour (although she wasn't and would most likely hold it against her forever) *I was out of order, purely jealous although I blew my chance when he came onto me earlier in the evening which I had ago at him for, for what reason I do not know. Thank god I won't have to see him again after embarrassing him and myself. What a twat!*

Thanks for coming girls. Officially graduated. Whoop! ☺

She group messaged the girls back rather than individually messaging everyone. Having been perched on the bar stool at the kitchen counter for the past 20 minutes a puddle had now formed beneath her as she had drip dried. As she stood to go back upstairs she remembered a text message she had dismissed from Jack in her inbox. She opened it expecting a short message; to her surprise she saw something more like an essay.

Hey Freya

Sorry I ran out on you the other night, I'm sure you think I'm a right dick after we shared such a great evening. I really enjoyed myself catching up, it's like no time has passed when I'm with you.

I lied to you though. Making you believe we would see each other again throughout the summer, we won't, I'm already back at camp. You probably think I used you for a shag, I know it's what it looks like but it was not intentional or planned. What we have in the past always brings back feelings which are too strong for us to just be friends. I wish it was different but it's not even as time passes. I know your thoughts on a relationship with me are out of the question, so I don't think we can hook up again as I'll always be wanting more.

If I'm ever about I'll give you a bell to catch up no strings attached but no sex time it's not fair on you or me or if you want we can just write to each other to keep connected.

You're beautiful and I'm jealous of any guy who gets to be with you. I wish things were different.

Good luck at your graduation.

Jack

xxx

Her stomach churned, the tea curdling in her stomach as she heaved causing her to be sick in her mouth. She quickly legged it to the bathroom where she spent some time hugging the toilet. She rinsed her face, brushed her teeth and felt slightly better. She shivered; as she threw on some clothes she felt upset Jack had gone again although she already had a feeling. She hated how she felt around him, hating the way she wouldn't allow herself to have a long-distance relationship with him, but knew it was for the best. Being friends is better than nothing, she believed. Unfortunately she'd most likely never get to see him draped in his army uniform again or be able to take it off his sexy body. She loved Jack but he would never be home where she wanted him.

Not feeling in the mood to talk, her mind confused, unknowing of what to reply, she replied:

Hi Jack

Thanks for the text. I enjoyed our time together too.

I agree with you, friends is better than nothing although it still makes me sad.

My graduation was good, feel worse for wear today though.

Write to me, you have my address.

Love Freya

xx

Placing her phone down she continued with her day, which consisted of comfy joggers and a baggy jumper, crap TV and a takeout meat feast pizza with a chocolate pudding. Having felt so rough she felt the need to replace all the sugar within her body and went against her usual diet, ordering the unhealthiest thing she fancied which she washed down with a bottle of Irn-Bru. She flicked through Netflix trying to find something decent to watch but trailer after trailer nothing was taking her fancy; she clicked play on a chick flick comedy which she would most likely fall asleep watching. Knowing she had completely wasted her day she promised herself that tomorrow would be a new day, she would make up for it, getting back on track with a long run.

As she enjoyed her food and sipped her drink she heard the front door. Placing down her pizza box from her lap she climbed from beneath her blanket, wiping her greasy fingers on her trouser leg as she made her way to the front door. *Who could be at my door at 11pm?* she worried. As it was too dark to look out of the window she opened the door slowly, unlocking the lock and chain with her long fingers completed by her shiny red nail polish coating her long nails. To her surprise Bradley stood before her, looking good and smelling as tasty as ever. He smirked at her. "Bradley? What you doing here?" she questioned surprisingly as she opened the door further,

"I was going to go out but I thought I would come and see your pretty face," he smiled.

"Come in," she requested as she moved aside, shutting the door behind him.

"Cute PJs," he laughed as he willingly walked in.

"Thanks," she laughed with a hint of embarrassment "I'm suffering today from last night," she explained as she walked him into the living room, climbing back into her warm spot, picking up her pizza box.

"A hangover? Eating greasy pizza and drinking fizzy drinks," he spoke as he grabbed a slice and poured a glass, making himself at home. "It must be bad," he choked as he spoke, eating at the same time.

"I know," she admitted. "Never again," she promised herself. "Were you going to the bar?" she asked, looking at the time.

"Ye, but it's boring in there now without you," he responded.

She returned the compliment with a laugh. "I'm sure," she smirked whilst taking a bite of her nearly cold dinner, each bite making her feel slightly better as she started to feel full.

Finishing off her mouthful she washed it down with a gulp of ice-cold water.

"So how was your graduation? It must have been good if you're hanging this bad," he asked as he made himself comfy in the space next to her, moving aside all the cushions that lay there.

"It was good, free drinks, free food, it was busy," she spoke, keeping the details to a minimum. "Oh shit," she blurted.

"What?" he asked.

"Argh, I was awarded the award of excellence by my tutor and there is a ceremony next week." She rolled her eyes, placing her head in her hands as she remembered. "Damn it!" she blasted.

"I want to say well done, but I'm getting the impression it's not a well done." He laughed.

"Long story short, I may have mentioned my lecture Matt before?"

"Ye I've heard of him once or twice, the hot one

as you would call him."

"Ha-ha, ye, him, well he came onto me last night and I basically told him to fuck off," she explained. "He ended up snogging Chloe and I kind of flipped out," she flushed. "Now I have to see him again," she stuttered.

"Oh dear, that will be a fun night for you then," he said.

"Maybe I'll get out of going or something," quickly trying to end the subject.

"I'm sure you deserve it though, aye?" he reassured her. "I get the impression, you need cheering up?" he asked with a sly look in his glistening eyes.

Without a response Freya knew exactly what he wanted, knowing he didn't need to ask.

Feeling unattractive as ever, she was somewhat impressed that her baggy clothes, no makeup and messy hair look still turned him on. She easily became in the mood to play. She moved aside her finished dinner, uncrossed her legs and leant over to him, placing a kiss firmly onto his lips. He responded quickly, she could already feel his hard on through his tight black jeans. Sliding on top of him she now straddled him in the corner of the sofa, his hands caressing her buttocks through her joggers which he so desperately wanted to remove. Biting his lip and nibbling his neck, she felt herself becoming wet within her pussy.

Hungry for sex, she undressed herself, lifting her top above her head, allowing her loose breasts to fall free. Her body warm, his face level with her tits, taking an erect nipple into his mouth, swirling his tongue it, biting hard. She gasped. He listened to her to moans as he played, cupping her breasts, stroking them. Removing his belt, she let his large cock escape from his jeans. Her hand grasped it, feeling so hard and thick. She ran her fingers along it, groping his balls, causing him to twinge, his breathing becoming heavier. She took a stern hold of his bulge and slid it back and forwards quickly. As he enjoyed his hand job he took his long fingers beneath her trousers to also find no underwear. Making his way to her pussy he placed two then three fingers into her juices as she groaned with delight. Hitting her g-spot, she was enjoying every move, becoming closer and closer to orgasm. "You're so good with your hands," she moaned as the words left her mouth. The aroma of sex filled the room. He removed her hand from his cock, grabbing her hips, placing his dick into her welcoming entrance. As it filled her she quivered. She ran her fingers through his waxed hair, riding him fast and hard.

Feeling every natural ripple of his dick she becomes flushed and speechless. She's breathing heavily, screams leave her mouth as she looks into his face, and she knows he is close to climax. He sucks on her large brown nipples as he pants with her. She rides him faster until her hips ache, her breasts bouncing with every movement. He places his hand on her ass, guiding her, and he thrusts harder and harder. "Yes, yes, yes!" she screams out as an orgasm flows through her body. She's now out of breath and her body's tired. Continuing to ride him, she places her hands onto his shoulders, she's gripping onto him hard, digging her nails into his flesh. He pulls her faster towards him, letting go as he explodes his juices into her. "Oh my god," escapes through his deep breathing.

Freya smiled down at him as their bodies slowed. Coming to a stop, she takes a deep breath and climbs off him, letting his cock fall onto his stomach covered in their juices. She stood naked, feeling hot, running her fingers through her hair. Although the sex was short-lived she felt better already. She walked into the kitchen, returning in a vest and shorts from her clean washing basket, now feeling too warm for her hoodie and joggers.

He sat looking, unable to move from the seat as he tucked his now floppy cock back into his boxers, fastening his jeans and belt back up. He climbed out the chair and grabbed his drink, draining it dry in a couple of large gulps. He looked at her, she looked back. "Thanks for coming round, I feel a lot better," she confessed.

"It's alright, I'm glad to have helped," he gushed with a smirk. "Can I grab another drink?" he asked, making his way into the kitchen.

"Help yourself, there's loads in the fridge," she responded.

Taking a seat back under her blanket, she noticed that she had missed half the film that was playing, not that she was into it anyway. Bradley returned, sitting back beside her. She made herself comfortable, placing her head onto her cushion; he pulled her feet round, placing them onto his lap which makes her heart flutter. *He can be such a gentleman; at least he hasn't just left like Jack did,* she thinks to herself. As the TV played nothing was said; within half an hour she had fallen asleep. He stood from the sofa trying not to wake her up, placed a blanket over her and made his way into the kitchen. As he searched through her drawers he grabbed a note pad and pen when he came to find one. He wrote:

I didn't want to wake you. Until next time ☺

Brad

Xxxx

Then switched the lights and TV off as he left the house, locking the door behind him.

CHAPTER 6

Chris

Opening her eyes she quickly sat upright as she realised she was still on the sofa. The smell of leftover pizza and Bradley's scent lingered within the room. Her wretched hangover was now gone, although her pizza has resulting in her feeling more bloated than ever. Rising from the sofa she made her way upstairs wondering when Bradley had left. Her hips ached a little as she walked from last night's sex session. She grinned, stretching her body as she walked into her bedroom. She undressed, looking for her workout clothes. As she spotted them on the dresser chair she put them on, as she really needed a workout. Her mind felt clear, feeling more positive than yesterday, feeling like she could manage a morning run. She ran down the stairs with a spring in her step, tied up her laces and grabbed her headphones from the kitchen window. Spotting the note from Bradley as she dashed past the unit, she smirked. "Yes, next time," she told herself. *Brad can be super cute sometimes, leaving me a note,* she thought. Pushing play on her playlist she shut the door and started to jog.

The air was fresh, the sun was just rising which made it cool enough to run comfortably. Having not looked at the time she assumed it was around 7am. Her feet struck the path one by one as she ran through several housing estates along to her music played, her breathing getting harder as she ran further. "Time 59 minutes 10 seconds, distance 6 miles," spoke through her headphones. Feeling she could continue she found herself running through the town towards the gym. She passed early shoppers and dog walkers who said, "Morning," as she ran towards them.

The clouds moved, opening up a blue sky, the sun shining down on her as it became warmer. *A good day for a sunbathe,* she thinks to herself. Sweat glistens across her brow and drips down her back; she continues. As the gym in is sight she slows and comes to a halt, enters the building, strolling towards the reception desk to find exactly who she is looking for.

"Hi stranger," Chris says as he walks around the desk to welcome her, standing before her with his ripped arms crossed against his body, his huge legs on show, she notices.

As she catches her breath, she grabs a paper towel and dabs herself dry.

"Hey, you're just the person I wanted to see," she smiles. "I need to start training properly, I have about five weeks if we can make a schedule?" she requested.

"No problem. When are you thinking?" he responded.

As Chris spoke she couldn't help but find herself staring into his gorgeous face, his eyes like the sky outside were staring right at her. His blond hair fell naturally amongst his face. She found herself grinning.

"OK, well university is done and dusted and I don't work at the moment, so my calendar is pretty empty," she confessed. "I could do with like, two workouts in the gym and wondered if you would also come running with me once a week, if you're a runner?" Freya questioned.

"You are keen. I'm free on Monday and Wednesday morning for a gym session and could fit in a run Saturday morning?" he said as he checked his diary.

"Perfect," she replied.

"Starting tomorrow?" he insisted.

"I'll be here – 6am?" she promised.

"I look forward to it," Chris responded with a friendly smile. "Right, I have a client coming in, I best get going," he said as a young girl walked through the doorway. "Enjoy your run home," he said as he walked towards her, making Freya feel jealous.

She smiled as she watched him walk away; his leg muscles were so thick and bulging and his back looked solid too. *He must be really strong,* she thought as she felt herself becoming hot under the collar. She clocked herself in the mirror. *Oh God, I'm like a beetroot, I've stood here looking like this as he looks like that,* she thought. She took a cup of water from the dispenser, downed it and made her way back out. As Chris' hot body was now penetrating through her mind she easily managed a further six miles home before the sun had reached mid-point.

She returned home, her legs felt achy after

achieving nearly half a marathon's distance; they shook as she stretched them off. Suddenly feeling lightheaded she grabbed some fresh orange juice from the fridge, poured a large glass and sipped followed by a pint of ice-cold water. Running always made her thirsty; she would most likely be drinking a lot for the rest of the day. As half of the day had already passed meaning less time to work on her tan, she quickly showered, threw on her bikini and made her way outside to her sun lounger where she stayed for the rest of the day. She refuelled her body throughout the day, making her feeling a lot healthier than yesterday. She relaxed.

The aroma of sun lotion and freshly cut grass filled the air along with the neighbour's BBQ cooking away; the smell of grilled sausages and roasted marshmallows made her feel hungry. Above her music she heard families and friends dining outside, clinging glasses and having a laugh alongside their kids running around having water fights and jumping in their paddling pools. She imagined that would be her one day, filling this large house with noise and memories.

The warmth on her skin had eased her aching muscles from her run this morning. As she made her way inside she moved aside her bikini strap to see her white lines, her skin now looking sun-kissed. She was blessed with genetics from Australian-born grandparents which resulted in her being blessed with a dark tan every year. All she had to do was look at the sun and everyone was envious. Following a good run, a day of healthy food and hydrating drinks she felt relaxed, she felt tired, but she felt happy. She went to bed following a yoga session looking forward to her workout with Chris in the morning.

*

Turning over, sprawled upon her bed, the duvet laid between her knees as she had become hot during the night, observing her clock, 5:29am it read, she had just beaten her alarm. Her skin felt warm to touch, stinging as it touched her sheets, feeling a little sore from her day in the sun. *Nothing a layer of after-sun won't ease,* she thought, although she wasn't looking forward to putting on her tight sports bra. She smothered aloe vera into her skin, she threw her hair into a messy bun, pulling her tight sports bra slowly over her skin as it hurt, causing her to wince. Covering her body with a baggy top with a pair of sports shorts and her gym trainers, she skipped out on breakfast as she disliked eating early. She grabbed a protein shake instead. She grabbed her keys and drove to the gym.

As she walked through the doors her stomach suddenly filled with butterflies. She didn't mind the upcoming gruelling workout, it was the thought of looking like a fool in front of her hot personal trainer.

Chris spotted her walk through the door; he stood almost immediately, grabbing his note pad. He walked towards her; she watched him as if he was in slow motion as she walked towards him. She felt somewhat excited to be spending £30 on one hour with a gorgeous specimen of a man, up close and personal, although getting sweaty in the opposite way she wanted, she cheekily thought. Just thinking about him made skin feel warm and her legs tingle.

"Morning Freya, how are we this morning?" he asked politely.

He's definitely a morning person, all smiley so early on, she thought. "I'm good, thank you, although I'm not quite as awake as you seem to be," she laughed.

"Argh well, you will be once this hour is up," he promised. "So over to the cross trainer we go," he requested as he asked about her week, smiling away.

After a quick ten-minute warmup Chris walked her into the studio to use the free weights, sandbags and kettlebells, commanding reps of squats, lunges and walking lunges several times over. Her legs felt like jelly, burning as she performed each set, her muscles working more than ever as sweat started to drip from her brow.

"My legs are killing," she giggled.

"Good," he laughed.

"My legs don't hurt like this when I'm running," she commented. "Is this how your legs are so big?" she quizzed as she looked up at him, raising from a low squat, holding a sandbag across her shoulders.

He noticed her eying up his bare legs and grinning. Freya seemed to think he liked the attention.

A vibration came from her phone which was placed on the floor. as it flashed she continued to work out. Chris picked up her phone, placing it in her hands having took a quick glimpse as it continued to ping. "Here, have a quick break, we're moving on in a minute," he told her.

Freya performed her last rep and let go of the sandbag with it landing behind her. She stretched out her arms, releasing the pressure from her elbows. She took her phone and eyed up the screen.

Email from Mr M Jones

Morning Freya

I am emailing you not as your lecturer but as you're associate, as I don't want to assume we are friends due to ruining that chance the other night.

No shit, Sherlock, she thought as she continued to read.

Congratulations on graduating.

I apologise for my behaviour and kissing your friend. I take the blame as I did drink too much which always ends in disaster, I have learnt my lesson now.

Anyway please accept my apology, if I did you wrong over the past few years I apologise for that also, this was not my intention, I was merely trying to be professional rather than friends, and with a good looking girl this can be hard.

Oh God, he's a sweet talker... Freya smirked.

I hope you have not lost your invitation to the award ceremony and I hope to see you there, acquaintance or friend either way.

Sorry

Hope your well

Matt

Freya quickly responded:

Hi Matt

I will be there. Let's not make it awkward, just forget about it all.

Sorry for going all psycho on you, I am sure it was not attractive to see.

See you on Saturday.

Freya

Her stomach sank but instead of dwelling on it she took her attention back to Chris. Thoroughly enjoying her workout, she grabbed her bottle, took a few large swigs and asked what was next.

"Take five," he insisted. As she did she perched on the tower of soft plyometric boxes. Chris sat on the edge next to her. He looked at her with a smile, making her feel uneasy.

"Tell me something about yourself then, so you have now graduated, how was that?" he questioned.

"Ha," she sighed, not wanting to recall the event. "The graduation was fine," she mumbled.

"Fine? Just fine? I thought graduation was this hyped up event everyone looks forward to?" he probed.

"Ye, me too, but it wasn't and I don't really want to talk about it or bore you with the details," she explained as she picked at her water bottle label as nerves ran through her.

"Sounds like it was a bust then, something to do with Mr Jones? I can only assume from your reaction when you opened your phone," he wondered, hoping she wasn't going to snap for being nosey.

"Err, yes it is," she murmured back. Her fingers touched her phone screen with a grin. *You're a bit upfront, aren't you?* she thought as she lapped up his attention, intrigued as to why Chris was so interested. "We haven't spoken since I made a bit of a scene, he just reminded me about my invite to the award ceremony, I kind of wish I didn't have to see him again," she explained.

"Aww, well if you need a body guard I'm free," he suggested, gazing into her eyes.

Is he suggesting a date? she questioned. "Are you asking me out?" she laughed, blushing.

"Kind of, you seem nice." He paused with a smirk.

"Nice?" giggling at him.

"You know what I mean, interesting, cool, I think we would get on." He was now getting himself tongue tied. "I want to spend time with you outside the gym if you would like?" he asked, smiling, with a look in his face, sure she wasn't going to turn him down. Obviously he was right.

"Ye, OK, that sounds nice, come with me," she requested.

"OK I will, glad that's settled," he spoke as he stood. "Let's carry on then, let's work those arms," he spoke as he stroked her triceps with a gesture.

The rest of the workout flew by, to her delight. As

flirty conversations were tossed back and forth she failed to notice the pain her body was being put through as she performed 15 minutes of burpees, push-ups, bicep and tricep sets; her whole body was now aching, glistening with a sheet of sweat.

Taking a firm roller he passed it to her, Freya giving a confused look up towards him. He sat on the mat beside her and showed her how to use it; she copied him with her eyes locked onto him, watching every move, feeling so hot for his big, large body. The tension between them heated up as they sat in silence. She finished stretching off her now heavy muscles and flopped onto the mat, a laugh escaping her as she let out a sigh.

"Oh my god, I thought I was strong," she questioned. "I'm shattered," she admitted. "How am I going to do that again in a few days?" shrugging her shoulders, wiping her brow.

"Oh you will and it will get easier, just eat plenty of the right foods and use the roller. Here, take this one." He handed it over.

"Thanks." Their fingers touching as she took it, he beamed toward her, wishing he could pick her tiny body up and make her scream for him. Letting out a large breath as he threw the image aside, "Right, I've got to go, I have another client now. Good job today, you have my number." He winked as he walked away.

What the fuck just happened?!?! she thought to herself as she watched him walk off. *A date?! A date?! What is wrong with me! Too many options, Freya, just too many!*

Her phone pinged again as she walked back to her car. Addressing the screen, she read:

Email from Mr M Jones

Thank you.
See you Saturday
Matt

With her mind playing on Chris she didn't feel the need to reply. After seeing a different side to Matt at the weekend she felt herself suddenly able to forget about him, plus not seeing him every day to ogle over also helped. She had started to question if she only fancied him because he was off limits when he was her teacher due to turning him down so easily when he gave her the chance. Instead she was now looking forward to seeing Chris again, even if the next time was another workout rather than their date. He seemed nice; although he was a lot more forward than she was used to he showed a genuine interest in her and the pure benefit of being a complete dream to look at.

*

It was late July and another week had passed by, much of which she had spent in the garden soaking up the 34-degree heat, which was considered a heatwave in England. The grass was a shade of yellow as no rain had touched the ground for weeks which was unheard of; the humidity in the air made it difficult to breathe as she ran. She was hoping for a little rain before her marathon just to make it easier.

Following several full-body workouts with Chris,

she was noticing her arms and thighs becoming more toned in such a short space of time. She was excited to see what kind of benefit this would have on her running sessions when she joined him for a long route.

The more she saw Chris the more she found out about him; it turned out he was the sort who liked to question everything. He constantly asked about her life, likes, dislikes, friends, family, which to her was different as no one else really made much of an effort or she never gave them the time of the day. To her surprise he seemed 'boyfriend' material which left her shocked at herself for even thinking about. She looked at Chris and didn't just see him as sex, although she did crave him. As they spent time working out she could feel the tension building between them. A feeling she hadn't felt for anyone but him lately, having not seen Matt or Bradley. Maybe this was a good thing. She found herself counting down the days to seeing him out of the gym on Saturday.

Saturday rolled round quickly. As she was pottering around she heard the knock at the door she had been waiting for. She rushed from the kitchen, slamming the door shut as she finished her last sip of orange juice. Looking at her running watch, it was dead on 7:30am. As she opened the door he stood there in his loose black shorts, Nike Air running shoes and a vest which sat perfectly between his defined back and shoulder muscles and his biceps looking solid. His blond hair swayed in the morning breeze. Just looking at him made her sweat, wondering how the hell he was single.

"Morning Chris," she stuttered.

"Hey, Ready to go? What we planning? Eighteen

miles?" he grinned.

Eighteen effin' miles!! she exclaimed to herself. "You must be joking, I've not ran that far! I can't do that! Twelve is my best so far," she responded, feeling anxious. "Well I think you can do further so we're trying 18. You do need to reach 26, right?" He spoke. "So prepare yourself for the next few hours," he commanded as he ushered her out of her doorway.

"OK, but get ready to be carrying me home," she giggled as she started her Garmin. They left the driveway jogging at a slow pace, allowing them to talk about what kind of week they had had. She was feeling more relaxed and less embarrassed each time she saw him; the more she learnt about him the more she liked him. He was funny, kind and caring as well as being utterly gorgeous.

*

As they neared 12 miles she felt herself continuously checking her watch; normally she would be nearing home by now, which seemed so far away right now. The thought of six more miles made her feel sick; her feet were starting to burn, her legs felt considerably OK but her mind was telling her to stop.

As she puffed she slowed to a stop and stretched her legs off. Taking a sip of water, wiping her brow she looked at Chris who had stopped beside her, not even looking like he was the slightest bit worn out.

"I can't do it, I'm done in, I told you," she panted, irritated with herself.

"Freya you can, this seems to be where you hit the wall. You tell yourself 12 miles and that's why you can't overcome it. You need to try and go further

81

each run, in a few weeks you're running 14 more miles than this, remember," he paused as she caught her breath. "You have got this." He stood before her with his hands on her shoulders, looking straight into her eyes.

She believed him, nodding her head as she sighed. He was good at spurring people on and it clearly helped him be good at his job. His body language changed as she stared him in the face; his body stepped closer and his head leaned in. She stood frozen although her lips responded as his touched hers, his hand on the back of her sweaty neck. As he stood tall she found herself tiptoeing to reach him. She ran her hands up his arms feeling the sweat pouring from his skin within her palms. He was hot to touch. She stopped at his biceps which her small hands didn't even fit around, not even half of the thickness. They were solid just as she thought. Her loins shook with excitement. She could taste the salt within his kiss, the smell of testosterone upon his skin arousing her. As their tongues entwined she found him to be a great kisser; she forgot all about her burning feet as she was in the moment. He stopped and stood back. His face lit up and her heels touched back down.

"Six more miles? Ye?" He spoke softly, smiling at her as he wiped her lips with his soft thumb.

"OK, I'll try," she hesitated, although she would much prefer to be doing something else with him. She smirked up at him.

They continued running; as her feet felt blistered she was surprised at how positive she found herself as she managed each extra mile. This was the first time she had run without music and with another person, she found having someone to talk to made running easier. She could listen to her breathing which also helped.

The street became busier as the hour passed. It was nearing midday, the sun was now warm, cars were driving by and kids could be heard in the nearby park. She was so caught up in how Chris had made her feel, a surprise kiss is a situation she hadn't encountered for years. Out in the open, in public. To oncomers they would appear as a couple, something she had also not experienced for a very long time. She was confused by how she was feeling. She didn't feel like just fucking him and leaving for the next guy, she enjoyed his company, what is this? Her mind raced. *I wonder if he talks to Louise about me, I'm going to ask her,* she thought.

As she caught sight of her street it amazed her how quickly the extra six miles had passed, with little struggle too. As she slowed towards her gate her legs felt tight and her feet tingled within her shoes, her abs ached and she started to cough every now and again as she stopped. She leant on her front door as she looked upon Chris, knowing she may have reached her limit for a while.

"See, you did it, in a good time too." He spoke proudly with a smug 'I told you so' manner.

"I know, I can't believe it, I'm shocked at myself. I don't feel as bad as I thought I would either." She nodded, too out of breath to talk. She downed her water empty as she opened the door, slipping her feet straight out of her shoes, stretching her toes out. She headed straight into the kitchen and prepared an energy drink for them both. Other than looking hot and sweaty he seemed like he could run another 18 miles, looking completely unfazed. *He must be super fit,* she thought. He took the drink and drank it as he watched her stretch out her legs.

He walked round the kitchen island and took her hand. Walking towards the patio door he unlocked the door.

"Lay on the floor," he instructed.

Looking at him, confused, "What for?" she queried.

"I'll help you stretch," he assured her.

"Oh OK." She blushed.

She laid flat on her back upon the grass. Raising her left foot, he took it, pushing it up straight, the stretch running down within her thigh muscle. Her face showed the pain but the release of the tension built within her muscle was satisfying. He placed her foot on his washboard abs as he stood above her leaning his body weight against her. She became anxious about her sweaty feet touching his body, too shy to say anything as he switched to the other leg. He helped her stretch and firm roll until her legs no longer felt tingly. Well, other than in between her legs anyway.

Holding out his hand down towards her, she grabbed it tightly; his grip was strong as he helped her to her feet. The tension between them needed to break, her mind going crazy at the idea of touching him, her body feeling like it was ready to erupt if she didn't become satisfied soon. As he started to stretch off his own body she walked into her kitchen, switching on her music which played through her Bluetooth speaker.

She undressed in the middle of the kitchen glad to be out of her clingy, sweaty clothes. Standing in a white Calvin Klein sports bra and thong allowing her sun-kissed tan to glow, she noticed Chris clock her as she stood with her body on show. He grinned and walked towards the door. She walked to the back door in his direction as she made her way to the ice-cold hot tub and she slowly lowered herself in. The cold touch to her skin instantly allowed her muscles to ease, the burning within her feet and aches within her body had disappeared. Chris watched her as he removed his footwear, leaving his shorts on, and climbed into the tub letting out a gasp, not expecting it to be so cold. His reaction made her laugh out loud. She turned up the water temperature a little so he could relax.

Her eyes were all over him as all sorts of images ran through her head, not knowing whether to act upon them as she so desperately wanted to continue their kiss from earlier. Chris made her stomach do somersaults; she couldn't read his body language which made her feel on edge. He seemed so perfect and she didn't want to ruin it.

In a daze, the water moves beneath her. Chris moving towards her, he kneels and places his arms either side of her, now unable to move. He opens his mouth to say something but she doesn't give him the chance – she grabs him from the neck, pulling him towards her, and kisses him hard. He responds quickly. They both feel the tension between them as they tongue and grope for what seems forever. His hand cupping her cold breast whilst the other is on her ass cheek, she's now sat upon him whilst tugging at his hair.

Oblivious to their surroundings, they don't seem to care about the noise they are making, the water swishing around out of the tub as they move. Her hands make their way to his cock; she discovers an almighty huge erection. *Obviously,* she thinks to herself, smirking beneath their passion. He twitches as she starts handling his cock, his touch becomes tighter on her body. Using his body strength he lifts himself and her out of the water onto the edge of the tub. Sliding her soaked thong aside and his shorts down he places his bulging cock inside her. She trembles, taking a breath. "Whao," she lets out.

"You OK?" he asks as he holds onto her waist, looking into her eyes. She nods, biting her lip hard, trying not to gasp. Until now she had never experienced a cock so large and thick, he felt deep within her stomach. Her hands held onto his large shoulders for support as she rode him slowly as her body adjusted for him. He allowed her to go at her own speed, making her relax; he clearly knows he is well endowed. She moved slowly at each thrust as his cock hit her g-spot deep within. Exhaling at each one. His hands on her hips guiding her to rock back and forth, it becoming more pleasurable as the ache within her tight pussy eased. Music still playing in the background, she had no idea what was on as her senses were currently unable to focus. The sun burning down onto their skin, the smell of the warmth filled the air. His eyes locked onto her, she felt completely in the moment.

Their bodies in complete sync with one another, slowly grinding as they kissed. Chris seemed to enjoy kissing, their tongues entwined. He moved his kisses from her lips to her neck to her aroused nipples, sucking amongst them. She grunted with each nibble, her pussy pulsing. As he drew close to orgasm he held his breath, trying to last longer. As he showed signs of reaching climax she rode faster and harder, bringing herself to peak with each thrust before he exploded inside her. His breathing increased, the expression of sex on his face.

"Oh my god," she wailed as she found her breath. Her tense arms released from his shoulders, relaxing behind his neck as she slowed. She pulled him forward and kissed his lips, biting as she let go. He smiled, looking at her in a daze. She felt completely full of sex, more than she ever had. She climbed off his now non-erect penis and sat back for a second, adjusting her underwear beneath the water, then stepped out of the tub. Chris stood tall now dressed back in his shorts and made his way into the kitchen.

"Can I grab a drink? That workout wore me out," he smirked as he walked around the kitchen unit, placing his hands on her back, kissing her shoulder blade.

"Of course, help yourself," she smiled back.

He made his way around the kitchen drip drying; he peered in the fridge and grabbed a bottle of Coke and poured an orange juice for her, assuming it was what she would want, and made his way back to the garden. She was laying on a blanket she had been sunbathing on yesterday looking up at the blue sky. Her eyes made their way to him as he stepped out the door with drinks in his hand. She observed every move he made, unsure if he was now going to leave like Jack and Bradley would have done by now. This was something she had got used to which deep down made her feel somewhat rejected. He placed himself onto the blanket beside her, passing her the drink. Taking it from his hand as their fingers touched she took a deep breath and took a sip. She lay next to him all afternoon, listening to music and talking to each other. Butterflies still swirled her stomach, this time not just from sexual desire, although her groin was still pulsing and feeling sore from his well above average sized penis.

As it drew closer to that evening's award ceremony Chris left to get ready back at home. He returned looking hot in a dark navy suit complete with brown shoes and a white shirt. She wore a long backless black dress with a slit down the leg, showing off her black suede heels. Her hair fell straight around her face, long down her back. Feeling nervous, she consumed a small glass of rosé, unsure of how she would feel as she saw Matt.

"My god, you look beautiful," Chris exclaimed as she walked down the stairs. "You must have a good personal trainer," he joked.

"Ha, thanks, are you sure I look alright?" she asked, performing a twirl.

"Yes, I'm sure," he responded, leering at her as he took her hand, placing a kiss upon it.

She grabbed her bag and they left for his car. She felt strange going out with a date as it was something she didn't do very often. *Nina would be impressed,* she thought to herself.

She grabbed her phone out her back and texted

her as Chris drove to the destination.

'Hey Nina, I'm going to my award ceremony with personal trainer Chris 'like a date' ☺ we're dressed in posh frock and suit completely looking the part, are you proud? Ha-ha.'

'Freya! That's great, I look forward to hearing about it make sure you take a photo, I hope you enjoy your evening but don't drink too much. Ignore Matt   ' she responded.

Freya smirked as she placed her phone back into her bag.

"Everything alright?" Chris questioned as he noticed her.

"Perfectly perfect," Freya gushed.

CHAPTER 7

One Too Many

"Your destination is on the right," came from the sat nav. It was dark outside with not many street lights lighting the road. They took the right turning which looked to be a large drive into a huge building.

"It's in a hotel?" he queried. She double checked the invitation, reading it out loud, reassuring him.

"This is right. Maybe it's in one of the conference rooms they normally have?" She spoke, shrugging her shoulders, now intrigued to find out. "It will probably also save people driving?" she added.

"Probably babes, it looks nice though and very posh. I now see why it's a black tie event," he replied.

Babes?! she thought. Having hated pet names she was unsure what to say to let him know she did not like this new nickname. After all it was their first proper date even if they had spent the day together. Surely that's too soon for 'babes'?! She tried her hardest not to frown upon it, until the next time anyway. Chris climbed out of the car and made his way round to her door; opening it, he took her bag and took her hand, guiding her to her feet. She climbed to her feet as her heels found the floor, adjusting her dress back to floor length as she took her bag.

"Thank you, such a gentleman," she admired.

He opened his arm out for her to hold, finding herself automatically holding onto him, feeling he was too intimidating not to. As they entered through the glass swivel doors she scanned the room, seeing several familiar faces, students and lecturers. A waiter came towards them holding a tray full of *Prosecco*-filled flutes towards them. She grabbed one, as did Chris.

"Thank you," she smiled.

They stood side by side sipping their drinks within the busy foyer, waiting to enter the main room.

"I'll be back in a minute," Chris spoke as he stepped away. She nodded as she observed the room.

The fresh-smelling canapés being served filled the air, her stomach rumbling at the thought of food. She was starving and really looking forward to the buffet later, her favourite kind of food. She took a canapé from one of the trays near her without hesitation as to what it was. Tasting the pastry filled with prawn and seafood sauce, she licked her lips, brushing off the crumbs, washing it down with her last swig of bubbles before she grabbed another one and another glass. She spotted a giant board near the hall entrance and walked towards it. Before her she read the table plan, enjoying how formal this evening was turning out to be, she scanned for her name, noticing each table was seated in subjects. Her name was sat right next to Mr Jones. *Obviously. Oh, this is going to be fun.*

Matt on my left and Chris on my right, a hot guy sandwich with me as the filling, she thought to herself, trying not to laugh as she sipped her second glass dry.

"Good evening Freya," she heard from beside her, glancing over her shoulder. Her sights set on Matt, dressed head to toe in a black suit, looking just as hot as he did at the graduation.

Holy fuck, he looks so hot. His lips look juicy, his hair's neatly done unlike ever before, he smells amazing. The scent of him sent tingles straight down her body to her groin causing her to sigh deeply, clearly still having a little something for him.

"You look amazing," he stated as he put another *Prosecco* glass into her empty hand. She took it willingly, wrapping her long fingers round it, touching his as he let go.

Taking a sip to help ease her nerves, she replied, "Hi Matt." She hesitated. "Thank you, you look good too," she added as she never got to tell him before.

"I'm sorry about before," he went to continue as she butted in. Taking a sip of what seemed to be orange juice, he listened.

"Forget about it." She paused. "Please." She smiled, not wanting to talk any more about it, feeling embarrassed about the whole situation.

"If you're sure?" he asked.

"I am sure, just promise me you won't go kissing any of my friends again," she smiled flirtingly, rolling her eyes.

"Ah, I promise." He shrugged with an apologetic expression. He continued to make general chit chat as she stood before her, asking about her summer holidays. He seemed happy to see her and was making quite an effort on his behalf. Little did he know she showed up with a date. For a minute she also forgot she was with Chris.

She spotted Chris walking towards her; from his facial expression he looked irritated, his eyes looking upon Matt as if he was trying to burst him into flames, the look of jealously cascading across his face. He was scowling at her, his body tense. She suddenly felt uneasy.

"Hi I'm Chris, Freya's date." He abruptly butted in their conversation, spoke glaring down at him as he stood a foot taller than him, holding his hand out for him to shake. His body language being enough to make any guy want to leave the conversation, she felt awkward. Watching him startle Matt with his rude behaviour, expecting him to leave, he surprisingly shook his hand completely unfazed by the huge guy she had decided to bring along.

"Hi Chris, I'm Matt, Freya's lecturer. It's nice to meet you." They shook hands.

"Ah Matt, I've heard all about you," he bluntly silenced him. Embarrassment flew through her body as his behaviour pissed her off. His envious attitude seemed to try and place ownership on her, making her regret bringing him along, although she was feeling relieved Matt wasn't fazed by him at all.

The doors opened to the hall. Matt had arrived without a plus one which resulted in her talking back and forth between both him and Chris. To her dismay they were not talking to each other. Luckily on the way over to the table he was caught up in another conversation with the other lecturers.

Observing the well-decorated room, it was more formal than she expected. Dimmed lighting and fairy lights were lighting the room. Dark red seat and table covers complement the room covered in shiny confetti pieces which she fiddled between her fingers. Each table in direction of the large stage, her heart skipped a beat with the dread of not looking forward to getting up there with everyone's eyes on her. She flicked through the booklet which was placed on her seat, finding the night's schedule and details of each award being awarded. Spotting her photo she read:

Freya Bell 100 percent deserves this award. Over the last three years she has showed commitment to each and every aspect of her degree. She is hard working and brings a smile to the room. Her skills, determination and commitment are at a level which cannot be taught. She will be an asset to any organisation when she starts her future career. Well done, Freya. It's been a pleasure working with her and she will be missed by the sports department.

She read it again and again, finding herself smiling every time. *That is the nicest thing anyone has ever said about me.* Although he was clearly trying to win back some brownie points following their previous disagreement. Feeling confused she sat stunned to silence. Did he really like her after all this time like he had suggested?

"By your face expression, I'm assuming you know he clearly fancies you," Chris spoke into her ear quietly over her shoulder.

Taken aback, she scowled towards him as anger surged through her.

"What is your problem!" she snapped, his sarcastic smile disappearing.

"Babe, it was a joke, but it's obviously true," he spat as he glanced over at Matt.

"Don't call me 'babe'! And no! It's not obvious!" She stood, throwing down the book, picked up the bottom of her dress and headed towards the ladies'. He sat stunned in silence as he sipped on his beer watching her walk out.

What the fuck! Jealousy! That's why he's single, she thought.

Exiting the room into the quite foyer, her ears buzzing from the loud ambiance, she hopes no one heard her outburst. Her heels thud on the tiled floor as she passes the bar and waiters, each observer looking upon her. She looks at no one and pushes the ladies' bathroom door open. Throwing her clutch down, looking in the mirror, she feels irritated and confused as to why she's so pissed off.

"Argh!" Catching her breath, she decides not to react like last time by getting drunk; instead she plans to get through the night as quickly as she can, ignoring both Matt and Chris.

After powdering her face and reapplying her lipstick she hears the microphone go. She takes a deep breath, a last glance in the mirror and calmly walks back through the foyer.

"Alright Miss?" a waiter asks.

"Yes, thank you," she smiles, looking over at a handsome guy wiping the bar.

Pulling open the door she sees Chris with yet another full pint of beer observing the room and Matt sitting next to her empty seat with his body completely facing away from Chris. Clearly he is trying to put off having to talk to him as he is happily speaking to others nearby. No one else is sat at their table. *What fun this will be.*

As she nears the table Matt looks up at her, unaware of what's just occurred and what he's being accused of by Chris.

"You alright?" he queries, quickly finishing his conversation to turn towards her.

"Ye," she responds.

Chris stands up, pulling her chair out for her, now acting like a gentleman, perhaps to show off in front of Matt or maybe his way of apologising, she didn't care. She sat holding her clutch on her knee as they shook beneath her with nerves as the awards commenced.

The room filled with applause as each student made it to and from the stage, feeling more anxious as time went on, which was passing by slowly. As she sat in silence she gazed around the room; it seemed most people were with a plus one, although seeing how bored Chris looked, she now regretted inviting him to come and wondered if she would have been having a better time if it was just her and Matt. Silence fell between each applause. Matt clearly noticed something had happened between her and Chris but looked hesitant to ask. Chris was making the most of the free bar which came as a shock to her due to his healthy lifestyle regime.

"I didn't expect you to drink this much?" she questioned, nearing to him.

"Can I not celebrate for you? It's a free bar and it's not like you seem to be making the most of it anyway," he shunned.

"Well someone has to drive home," she snapped back as she realised he would now be over the limit. "You need to slow down before you actually ruin the night, and the whole day we have had together," she spoke, holding her teeth together, trying not to speak so loudly others would hear.

"I'm not doing anything, calm down."

"You're drinking too much and making rude comments which are making me feel uncomfortable," she clarified.

"Oh sorry, would you rather me leave you here with your boyfriend?" he remarked with a slur as he gazed into her face, his words becoming louder as he spoke.

Matt turned his body toward them both, now becoming part of the conversation. "What was that?" he questioned.

Freya, looking upon him, turned her body towards him slightly, placing her hand on his shoulder. She spoke into his ear, allowing him to hear her over the loud atmosphere.

"Nothing, he's had too much to drink, don't worry about it," she spoke, starting to feel embarrassed. Matt, glancing at Chris, stared back, curious of his behaviour, clearly having heard her comment.

"No I haven't!" he hissed at her. "I said maybe I should leave you two together as you clearly fancy her." He spoke nastily, looking down at them both as he rose from his chair. His body looking large above them, they stood to his level, trying not to make a scene.

"Stop it, Chris!" Freya exclaimed.

"I think you need to back off, there is nothing between me and Freya, she is my student," Matt responded in defence. Chris' body drew closer to Matt's. She stood between them, trying to usher his body back with her hand on his chest.

"Please stop it, Chris, you're drawing attention to yourself," she commands as people start to turn their heads towards them.

"If you have a problem, mate, then it's time for you to leave," Matt insists.

"I am not your mate, it's obvious you fancy her, look at this shit you have wrote," holding up the book. "Well she's my girlfriend, not yours, so you can back off," he continues, everyone now staring at them. Freya, completely embarrassed, was unsure of what to do or where to look.

"Chris, just back the fuck off! I never said I was your girlfriend," she scolds him.

"Excuse me, sir, can I ask you to move this away from the ceremony and calm down?" hotel security suggested calmly towards Chris, moving the chairs out of the way, allowing him to move. Chris barged his way out the room.

"Sorry Matt," she apologised. "Sorry about this,"

she reassured the worker, deeply apologetic.

Matt stood watching her move as she followed Chris out of the room. "Freya you haven't got your award?!" Matt worried.

"I'll be back, I'm sorry," she spoke.

"What a fucking prick," she heard Matt say to a colleague as they walked out. She didn't look back.

Outside Chris was stood leaning against the wall drinking a beer. He looked up at her as she made her way towards him, not even looking sorry. Freya felt upset, angry and embarrassed.

Trying to talk calmly, she spoke. "I don't understand what your problem is, we were having a good day and now it's ruined. We're on our first date and all of a sudden you're claiming I am your girlfriend and acting all jealous," she questions, looking into his eyes.

"We were until you and your boyfriend started flirting. It pissed me off!" he exclaimed.

"Hang on, me and Matt have hardly spoke all night," she confusedly asked.

"It doesn't take a genius to see what's going on," he remarked, finishing his beer. A heated discussion went on for what felt forever. Everything she was saying resulted in snide, immature comments and accusation; she felt she had enough.

"It's clear your major downfall is jealously and being way overprotective, you have made up this whole situation in your mind and you are not dropping it. I've had enough now," she spoke in a pissed-off tone. He looked at her, falling mute.

"Chris, go home, today has been ruined, I'm going back inside," she directed him.

"Back to him." He pointed towards Matt who was now walking over with a look of concern on his face.

"Are you alright, Freya?!" he asked, not even wasting effort to look at Chris.

"She is fine, thanks for your concern," he spoke for her.

"Actually, no I'm not, the night's been ruined. I have clearly missed my award and I just want you to leave," she spat towards Chris then looked away.

Matt stepped towards Chris to escort him towards the taxis outside the building.

"Look mate, you have had too much to drink, you have made a scene and you're upsetting Freya and others by your shouting, just go home."

"Don't touch me." He moved his arm aggressively away from Matt, giving him a push, dropping his glass which shattered on the floor.

"Matt, leave him, let's just go inside," Freya spoke, upset.

Matt moves to turn away from Chris when he is stunned by a fist hitting him across his jaw out of the blue, followed by another attacking punch to his left side, knocking him from his feet tumbling into Freya. She loses her balance but manages to stay upright by grabbing onto Matt, which stops him from falling over. Chris stands there ready for a response with his fists held tightly closed looking pleased with himself. Matt checks Freya is alright and sorts himself out, looking dazed, holding his jaw but does not retaliate.

"Chris! What the fuck!" she bellows.

"I see the way he's looking at you…" he butts in.

"You have serious issues, mate, there is nothing going on here," Matt speaks, trying to hold his cool.

"Chris, fuck off, this is stupid, and you're acting like a child," she snaps at him as he stood staring at her. "Come on, Matt, let's go back inside," she prompts as she grabs his hand, taking him inside, not looking back at Chris as she turns her back to him. He doesn't follow.

"Are you alright? I'll get you some ice, I'm so sorry, I don't even know how this has happened," Freya hysterically spoke.

"Hey, chill out, I'm fine," he responded as he found his voice. He leant with his back against the bar holding ice wrapped within a cloth upon his face. "I'll have a lager please, mate," he probed towards the bartender.

"Of course, sir," he replied as he poured him a pint.

"I'll have a large glass of wine too," she ordered, now feeling stressed.

"So that tool's your boyfriend?" Matt asked with a laugh, seeming quite calm for someone who had just been punched round the face twice.

"No, he's definitely not my boyfriend. Today was our first date and after that it will be the last one too." She paused. "I met him at the gym, he's my personal trainer," she explained as she sipped on her wine.

"Argh, explains the muscles," he laughed.

"Well he seemed alright until he saw you, although I had been wondering why he was single, ha-ha."

"Come on, I'm a guy and if I looked like him I wouldn't be jealous of anyone," he laughed as he sipped his beer.

"You're a good-looking guy, I can see why he was worried," she blushed as she complimented him with a smirk.

"Ha, well I apologise for being so dashing," he joked, looking at her as he continued holding his face.

"It's alright, I hated the way he called me 'babe' anyway," she confessed, shrugging her shoulders as she finished her drink before asking for another one.

He raised himself from the bar stool; the side of his face was red and swollen, sure to bruise by tomorrow, although he still looked gorgeous in her opinion. He looked down towards Freya with sorrowful eyes, showing he felt bad for yet another night involving him had been ruined.

"Come on, let's go back in, hopefully you won't have missed your award." Moving his body from the bar, placing his hand on Freya's back, he guided her to start walking towards the room. His hand felt warm against her skin, sending shivers down her spine. *Maybe the rest of the night won't be so bad after all,* she thought.

As they entered the dark room, the awards were still being handed out. Quickly making their way to their seats they sat back down. He scanned the programme as the next award was given out.

"You haven't missed yours, luckily," he smiled,

feeling relieved.

Freya felt more relaxed as the evening went on. She finally got to enjoy a plate of tasty food as drinks were flowing. She and Matt conversed and laughed with one another as well as others from the surrounding tables. With Chris and his antics falling to the back of her mind she started to enjoy her evening, other than a feeling of guilt every time she looked at Matt's face where his jaw lines were now swollen, although he was doing well to hide his pain every time he spoke.

*

"This next award has been chosen by Mr M. Jones from the sports department... For her sheer determination to succeed. This student is hard working and a pleasure to work with. With high standard of work she will be sure to excel in her career, let's hear it for Freya..." Her knees buckled under the table as she heard her name through the microphone. Matt took her hand and helped her from her seat, letting go as she rose. A combination of high heels and feeling tipsy was not the best idea, considering she promised herself she wasn't drinking that much tonight. Everyone now staring at her as they clapped, her heart rate rose as she panicked about falling flat on her face, trying not to make eye contact with anyone and becoming flushed with embarrassment. She held the bottom of her long dress as she slowly made her way up onto the stage. Collecting her award from the presenter, she shook their hand with a 'thank you' as photographs were being taken. She made one glance up to the crowd with a smile, her eyes focusing straight on Matt. She hated him so much right now for making her get in front of all these people as well as lusting over him as he sat there smiling at her with a shiny bruised face. She quickly made her way back down towards her table. Clinging onto her award she grinned towards him and placed it on the table, letting out a deep breath with thanks it was over.

"Well done Freya, I sincerely mean it. Even if you don't think you deserve it." He hesitated. "In honesty I am pissed at myself for making you think I disliked you as a student and that I may have been a dick at times. If it's any consolation it is far from the truth," he said, looking at her as she sat on the edge of her seat.

"Thank you, Matt. I'm going to get a drink, do you want one?" she asked.

Stunned at her basic response, he responded, "Ye, go on then, I'll have another pint."

Having now passed the tipsy phase she continued as the night went on, sipping on *Prosecco* and the odd shot of bourbon every time she approached the bar. She decided to celebrate in style along with everyone else.

*

The evening was coming to an end, the room was starting to clear out of drunk students and their friends and family members. Matt had spent some time with her at the table as well as socialising with others around the room, enjoying the odd few pints here and there.

"Freya," Matt spoke as he gently pulled her towards him from the dance floor where she had spent most of the last hour dancing away to the cheesy classics.

"It's time to go, they're clearing the room out." She didn't respond. Not knowing if she heard him, he prompted her again. Having watched her dance and drink the night away, it had become obvious she was going to be hard work getting home.

Freya's face turned close to Matt's. "No, Mr Jones, it's not time to go, come and dance," she slurred as she tried pulling him onto the dance floor. "Anyway my lift home left hours ago," she chuckled as she then realised she wasn't getting home unless he paid a fortune for a taxi.

"I gathered that was the case," Matt spoke, holding onto her hands. "Come on, let's go." He took her to her seat where she slumped into the chair, suddenly hit by the amount of alcohol she has consumed, no longer aware of her surroundings. Lifting her from her seat, placing his arm around her body, holding her upright, he grabbed her shoes, bag and award as he left the table. She wobbled her way to the entrance as Matt pressed the elevator button.

"Freya, you can stay in my room upstairs, I'll take you home tomorrow," he arranged, not even considering putting her in a taxi on her own.

"Ooo in your bed, I've wanted that all year," she slurred, smiling at him. "You hot teacher," she bellowed as she struggled to stand, finding a wall to lean against.

Matt laughed saying nothing back. Onlookers watched as they saw the state of her, asking if he required any help. He politely declined.

Being completely sloshed, she sat on the floor of

the elevator, going completely limp on him as he tried to stand her up. He had no choice other than to carry her to his room. With his hands full he struggled to open the door with the digital key but eventually made it in, his arms aching from the dead weight of Freya who was conscious but sleeping for now. Placing her on the bed, pulling the quilt on top of her, she lay there with her dress screwed up, her hair a mess, looking somewhat peaceful in her drunken state. She didn't move.

Taking the glass from the side table he filled it ready for her when she woke. He sat down on the armchair, taking off his shoes and jacket, sat back, slumped into the chair watching Freya as he drank a pint of water. He relaxed properly for the first time during the evening. Holding his cold glass on his now bruised face, he sighed. *She's worth it,* he thought, falling asleep shortly after.

*

Matt woke early, his body aching from an uncomfortable few hours' sleep in a small chair. The thought of lying next to her crossed his mind. Rising out of the chair, he gazed upon Freya who was fast asleep in the same position he placed her in. Not wanting to wake her he grabbed his gym clothes from his bag, leaving the room, quietly heading for an early morning workout.

Feeling refreshed after a few hours working out in the gym and some time in the sauna, Matt was thankful he was not suffering from a headache this morning. After keeping an eye on Freya all night most of his drinks were wasted although it was probably for the best as he now had to drive her home. With it being the last time seeing her he didn't mind an extra few hours with her, especially as she didn't seem to take to his efforts last night when he was trying to express his feelings for her. Maybe he could try again later if he was given the opportunity. Knowing she would be struggling this morning he made his way back to the room, collecting some breakfast for them both along the way in hope she was now awake. As he opened the door he placed the selection of continental cereal, croissants, fruit and juice onto the unit to find her still sleeping. He shut the bathroom door behind him as he headed for a shower. Freya woke with a startle. She opened her eyes wide to observe her surroundings; her mind felt boggled, currently unaware of where she had ended up for the night.

She pieced together the argument with Chris, her award and a night full of drinks and dancing which her migraine was an obvious result of. Her memories failed her from when she left the table to ending up in what she had worked out to be a hotel room.

"Oh shit, I hope I haven't done anything stupid," she spoke out loud. She slowly sat up as her body felt fragile. She climbed from beneath the quilt to find herself still wearing her dress. The soles of her feet stung from dancing in her heels for the majority of the night, her stomach churning with hunger and the taste of bourbon filling her mouth. Looking in the mirror, she found her hair to be a complete mess along with smudged make-up from a deep sleep. *Oh my god, what a state,* she thought as she placed her face into her hands, taking a breath for five minutes, trying to escape the buzzing within her ears from the loud music throughout the night.

Spotting the breakfast placed on the unit, she poured herself a glass of apple juice along with a tea as she took bites of the croissant after spreading it with jam. Enjoying every taste, she slowly started to feel more human as she refuelled her body.

The bathroom door opened, giving her a fright, having completely assumed she was alone having not noticed anyone's clothes or items within the room. Jumping out of her skin, she spilled her drink as her eyes locked onto a fresh-looking, well-groomed Matt. Her heart sank knowing full well how awful she currently looked. Three years of ensuring she looked good at university now seemed such a waste of time as he looked upon her with a humiliated look written across her face.

"She finally rises, does she?" he smirked as he placed his bag down, sorting through his stuff. "You have been asleep for hours, I didn't want to disturb you, although I do need to check out soon," he explained, looking at his watch reading nearly 10am.

Her head filled with questions to help fill in the blanks, although she found her voice to be silent as she sat staring upon him. He smelt amazing.

"How did I end up here?" The words slowly left her mouth as she stood leaning against the unit, noticing his bruises. The memory of him being double punched by Chris played hell on her.

"Well after you collected your award you drank, you danced, you enjoyed yourself. I knew you had no way home and I wasn't comfortable putting you in a taxi on your own in a drunken state so I carried you up here to let you sleep it off," he explained.

"Oh God, how embarrassing, I am so sorry." She felt stupid, hiding her face in her hands.

"Don't be, I'm just glad your night wasn't ruined after the whole Chris drama," he reassured her.

"What a prick, aye, and your face looks sore, I'm so sorry." She paused, feeling mortified. "Although you seem to carry it off quite well," she laughed. "Makes you look more rugged," she flirted.

"I wouldn't worry about it, I've had worse," he said as he looked upon his shiny bruise which still hurt with every movement of his face. "It's a good job it's the summer holidays really." She smiled, still feeling awful having caused him to get punched on her behalf.

"Can I ask, I didn't say or do anything inappropriate last night, did I?" She blushed as she sipped her tea.

"Err, no, not that I can recall," he responded with a smile. Her comment in the lift he decided to keep to himself.

"Oh thank God." She leant back with relief, now sitting on the unit. He felt unsure of whether it was a 'thank God I don't want to go there' or a 'thank God I didn't ruin my chances'. He was happy to go with the second option. He hoped she liked him like he liked her. "Thanks for the breakfast, I needed it, I feel loads better now."

"No worries, it was included, I grabbed it on the way back from the gym."

"Oh, check you out. I seriously need to stop drinking, I would love to be feeling as fresh as you right now," she laughed as she ate another handful of grapes.

"Well someone took my bed and I had backache from sleeping in the chair, so I killed some time whilst you slept," he went on.

"Well now I feel awful. I ruined your evening, I got you punched, you ended up babysitting me and you slept in an uncomfortable chair," she said with her head in her hands.

Matt stepped towards her, sitting beside her as he took some fruit. He looked so hot, she would do anything to kiss him right now, her body tingled at the thought of being about to touch him. Knowing it would cross a boundary she fought every temptation. "Call it even, ye?" he asked, referring to her graduation.

She smiled. "Ye, OK then."

"Right, I hope you don't mind but I have to check out, do you want a ride home?" he offered, hoping she wouldn't decline.

"I don't mind, I can always get a taxi if it's out your way." Although she was desperate to spend more time with him.

"No, it's not, let's go," he ordered as he grabbed his bags.

Freya quickly washed her face, removing the smudged make-up from beneath her eyes, and sorted her hair out. She looked slightly better, although still dressed in last night's clothes she felt she was performing the walk of shame and hoped not to bump into anyone she knew on the way out. Looking forward to changing her clothes, she grabbed her shoes and bag and left the room behind him, grabbing a mint on the way out.

CHAPTER 8

Matt

Now showered and feeling fresh she enjoyed her car journey home with Matt. Having enjoyed conversations with him plus the odd playful banter, it turned out Matt was easy to talk to and was actually really nice. She now felt awful for calling him a dick all this time especially considering he looked after her all night, whereas Chris turned out not to be at all concerned about her getting home, having received no messages from him.

As she walked down the stairs post fell through the letterbox, landing on the welcome mat. She picked it up and flicked through the pile of junk mail, phone bills, and came across a handwritten envelope, something she never received, written in handwriting she didn't recognise. Making her way into her kitchen she opened the envelope, finding pages of A5 sheets of handwriting signed by Jack. Sudden butterflies swirled within her stomach; she perched on a bar stool and started to read.

Hi Freya

I hope you are doing ok and do not hold any grudges against me about the way I left it between us. I'm doing well, keeping busy as usual, I would love to talk to you every day, and ever since I've seen you I miss you. I haven't stopped thinking about you since I left, I know it's not what you want to hear but I need to get how I feel off my chest as it's eating me up inside and keeping me awake at night.

I can still smell the scent of your body and feel the touch of your hands. I feel like my body is yours although we are not together. As I lay at night surrounded by silence I imagine what I would be doing to you if I was home. These thoughts make me mad as I know by the time I'm home it will be too late and I'm sure some other guy will have you. As I write this I can't help but get turned on. Imagining your body close to mine, feeling your soft red lips against mine, nibbling at them the way you do, biting them like I don't enjoy. Your dainty hands are in my hair pulling at each strand. Your legs wrapped around my body as my hands hold your toned peachy ass in them tight jeans. Your big breasts are held tightly within your red lace bra, I'm kissing your soft skin using my teeth to move aside the lace taking your erect nipple in-between my teeth, your groaning, you like it. My dick is so hard and needs to be held tightly by you, I need you to caress it like you own it, fast, slow, hard or soft I don't mind. I want to come over your body. I want to fuck you hard looking into your come to bed eyes, watching your cheeks flush hearing you moan, asking for more bringing you to orgasm. My body is going crazy, I need to have you.

I don't see how I can ask you to wait for me but if I had one wish it would be for you to hold out for me. I'm wondering whether your even reading this, if your body wants mine like mine wants yours. I want to snuggle you at night and fall asleep holding you.

It's lights out now.

Keep in touch

Jack

xxx

She sat staring at the words, reading them over the over. Feeling slightly aroused she felt her pussy tingle; the urge to pleasure herself surged through her body. Placing the letter down she made her way to her bedroom, tingles running through her inner thighs, her pussy feeling wet. Her mind playing with the words from Jack's letter, imagining everything he wrote. Grabbing her tingly durex lube out her knicker drawer she undressed her bottom half and laid on her bed, placing some lube on her three forefingers and starting rubbing her clit. The thoughts of Jack touching her, his hands on her warm skin, the natural scent of his hair in her face as she straddles his lap, taking it all it as she inhales. Their lips touching gently as he is taking control. The thoughts run through her mind as she strokes her wet pulsing pussy; she circles her clit as she plays with her breasts. Biting her lip as she becomes more aroused, nearly reaching climax. Imagining the sound of Jacks groans as he thrusts into her deeply, holding onto her hips tightly as he's tugging at her hair. His hands all over her. The image of him dressed in his uniform enters her mind, enough to send her to orgasm. Her fingers moving gently but fast across her clit, tension builds within her body as she reaches climax, her area feeling warm and sensitive. Her body trembles as she lets out a breath and smiles to herself, now feeling relaxed from head to toe.

Laying upon her bed for five minutes, she got lost within her thoughts about the current situation she was in with men. Knowing she had three too many options, she knew she had to cut ties with some of them as she had slowly become more aware of how quickly she went from one to the other. She found herself hesitant as to which ones, as she liked them all for different reasons. She knew she needed to reply to Jack but what to say was the difficult part. Jack was always going to be the one that got away for obvious reasons, although to her it was never going to work out. Although the other men in her life were also not great choices, a 22-year-old booty call, Matt who she would never see again but lusted over the thought of him, and a heartthrob who had turned out to have jealousy issues. On that note she remembered she had received a text from Chris she hadn't read. After sorting herself out and making her way back downstairs she grabbed her phone and opened her text.

Morning

I hope you're ok.

I'm sorry about last night, please forgive me.

I'll pop by yours later on around 1.

Xx

Giving a huge sigh she looked up at the clock — 12:45, it read. *Oh God,* she thought, dreading the thought of seeing him. Quickly running back upstairs she changed into her workout clothes for her long run. She made herself look a bit more attractive. Even though he turned out to be a jealous twat she still fancied the pants off of him and didn't want to look unattractive. Short black running shorts, a tight purple sports bra underneath a grey sports vest was all she needed to pull off a good look in her opinion, especially as he already fancied her anyway. Scraping her long shiny hair back into a high ponytail, he knocked on the door.

She made her way down the stairs and opened it to Chris standing there with a regretful expression and a bunch of flowers.

"Hey." He paused. "I'm sorry," he expressed as he passed her the flowers. "Please forgive me."

She took the flowers. "Roses, my favourite," she responded with a smirk. "It doesn't change anything though, we were having such a good day and then you completely ruined it by punching Matt for no reason!" she exclaimed still feeling pissed about it.

"I know, I know, I'm sorry," he spoke waiting for an invitation in. Feeling fired up, she was strong enough to speak her mind.

"Look, Chris, I like you but I don't want commitment right now and you're trying to move way too fast and I feel smothered by it." She paused. Chris stood staring at her in silence, to her surprise. "We had a nice time, as short as it was, but I don't think it's going to work between us," she admitted.

His face dropped as his smile vanished from his face. He backed away from the door frame with the same irritated face he had on yesterday. Unsure what was coming she stood waiting, ready to shut the door.

"You ended up in bed with him didn't you," he snapped.

"What? No I didn't. What the actual...?" she retaliated.

"Don't deny it," he butted in, speaking louder.

"Chris, lower your voice, I have neighbours. I did not end up with him. For your information I ended up passed out on the floor with no ride home thanks to you. Yes, he brought me home but that was it. Get over it, get over yourself." Feeling angry, her palms started to sweat. Feeling like she had to defend Matt, she now wanted gone of Chris.

"I am not doing this. I don't date jealous guys and I haven't done anything to even argue with you about. Don't expect me back at the gym and delete my number." She slammed the door, locking it without giving him any opportunity to respond.

What the actual fuck is his problem?

"Arrrgggghhhhh!" she let out.

Walking into her living room she watched Chris get in his car, shutting his door with a slam, driving off, revving his engine. Feeling glad he had gone she scrolled down to Louise on her phone and called, reaching voicemail.

"Hi Lou. Hope you're alright. Just to let you know it didn't work out between me and Chris. Long story short, he is the jealous type. Not the guy for me. Catch up soon please, love you, bye," she rambled and hung up.

Feeling tense, she grabbed her headphones and left the house. A long 20 miles later she made it home with sweat dripping from her body. She grabbed a towel and dabbed herself off. Stretching her muscles off as sweat poured from her skin, she could taste the salt amongst her lips. Her legs burning, a shade of red from both the sun and overworked muscles, her shoulders also aching. I could really do with a full-body massage, she thought. Knowing the last few miles were a struggle she became concerned about reaching her goal, especially now she didn't have a personal trainer to spur her on with his bulging biceps.

Placing her headphones and phone down, she grabbed an energy drink, sipping at it whilst she caught her breath. Reading her Garmin, seeing her progress, she felt proud of her achievement even if it did hurt. "Who needs a personal trainer anyway? I've got this," she said out loud, feeling motivated.

Following a refreshing shower she threw on some baggy jeans, a comfy t-shirt and ran a brush through her towel-dried hair. Popping a bottle of wine and a bag of Doritos into her large handbag she climbed into her car and drove to Chloe's for an afternoon of girl talk, alcohol and crappy food. Walking in late, she could already hear conversations in full swing; the hallway was filled with the aroma of Mexican spices, much to her delight. Inhaling the smell of her favourite food she made her way into Chloe's large kitchen, laminate flooring beneath her bare feet making them feel cold. On the wall hung a large white 4K TV matching the shiny white units. Complementing the area sat a large 12-seater table mid-centre of the room where she held meetings with her fashion designers and plenty of dinner parties. Sofas filled the walls all draped with leopard-print throws and a completed back wall made of huge glass windows and doors overlooking a large garden leading down to the canal where they often walked.

"Hiiiii!" Freya said excitedly.

"Here she is." Louise stood, giving her a squeeze. "How are you, my lovely?"

"Good thanks, sorry I'm late… managed a 20-mile run," she boasted.

"That's fantastic, you're getting there," Chloe spoke with a smile.

"You're going to smash that marathon," Nina added with confidence.

"Thanks, I hope so," she said as she poured a glass of wine, took a nacho from the hot pan just removed from the oven and sat straight down.

"Right, now we're all here!!!!" Nina spoke, gaining everyone's attention.

Each of them looked right at her, waiting for her to break the sudden silence.

"I'm getting married!!!!" she squealed with sheer enjoyment, her eyes beaming with joy.

"Oh my god!! Congratulations, let me see your ring." Chloe grabbed her hand. "Look at that diamond, it's gorgeous." They all observed her new shiny platinum Tiffany engagement ring which sparkled within the light.

"Congratulations, how exciting, I knew it was going to happen soon," Louise said as she gave Nina a cuddle and a kiss on the cheek.

"I love a good wedding, something to look

forward to! Congratulations Nina, I'm super happy for you," Freya added with large grin. "I can't wait for the hen party," she laughed.

"Thanks girls, I've been so eager to tell you all."

The girls spent hours throwing back and forth wedding and hen party ideas; bottles of wine were now empty and large amounts of Mexican food and snacks had been consumed.

Freya was feeling tipsy. "Seems I'll be walking home," she giggled. Her phone buzzed, the screen lit up, a nosey Louise gazed upon it.

"Oh, a message from Jack and an email from Mr M. Jones," she beamed, giving Freya the eyebrow of curiosity with a nudge.

"Ow, Freya, what's the gossip with your men?" Chloe asked as they all grabbed snacks and waited for her to speak.

She giggled. "Well it's a long story, but I would rather not get into it right now."

"What? That's not like you," Nina admitted as she elbowed Louise with a concerned grin.

"Ye, I know, but right now it's more confusing than fun, I don't know what's happened to my love life. Chris ended up being a complete jerk. He's been the first guy I actually considered dating and now he's completely put me off a relationship." She paused.

"Oh that's shame, he always seemed nice when I see him in the gym," Louise questioned.

"Ye, I know, but now I see why he is single," she admitted.

"What about Matt?" Nina asked.

Freya beamed at the thought of him. "Matt's a really nice guy and super gorgeous, did I tell you Chris punched him in act of jealousy?!"

"What! No!" they all exclaimed, eager to know more.

"At the awards ceremony Chris became jealous of him for no reason whatsoever. We were arguing outside, Matt came over to see if I was alright and he punched him twice right out the blue," she spoke shrugging her shoulders.

"What a dick!" Chloe snapped.

"Poor Matt," Louise spoke. "Especially as Chris is huge!" she added.

"Ye, I know, he handled it well but he looked terrible yesterday."

"Yesterday? Something happened between you?" Nina queried.

"I wish. I drank too much, passed out and woke up in his hotel room. He looked after me and brought me home. With the state I was in I'm pretty sure I have put him off me for good, ha-ha." She giggled, wishing the story was more exciting to tell, taking a sip of her wine as everyone else listened on.

"There's always Bradley from the bar?" Chloe asked.

"Well we hooked up but I think we both know it's just for fun. Actually, thinking about it I haven't heard from him since I last saw him," she quizzed herself. She had become used to the odd texts here and there.

"The young one from the pub?" Louise butted in.

"Ye," she responded.

"I've seen him several times in the bar with the same blonde girl," Louise replied.

"Oh, like a girlfriend?" Freya shrugged off, feeling slightly gutted.

"I think so, she seems nice and he seems to like her," she went on.

"Good for him," Freya added.

"That leaves Jack then?" Louise laughed.

"We had a great time together, he then texted me saying we shouldn't hook up anymore as he will always want more. I received a letter in the post from him saying how he's in love with me and can't stop thinking about us being together which he knows I won't change my mind on. I need him here if he wants a relationship. I know I'm being stubborn but I just can't do long distance. I haven't replied to him yet."

The room fell silent for few seconds as they all sipped their drinks, noticing Freya had become slightly mellow. "Maybe reply to the letter? Tell him how you feel?" Nina told her.

"I don't feel anything. Well, I do but I don't know what it is. He makes me feel numb when I think about the past, it hurts too much," she explained.

She stood up mid-conversation, helping herself to a glass of water, now feeling the need to sober up. Having now discussed her love life she felt miserable over the fact that she couldn't just be like Nina and settle down.

"Why not ask Matt out? You have liked him for three years and he seems to like you," Chloe shouted to her across the room. "He is a good kisser too," she laughed, making Freya choke on her drink with a giggle.

"Ha, maybe," she finished. "Right, I'm going to get a move on." As she looked at her watch reading 1:15am Freya stood, pulling on her Converse with a wobble.

"You sure you can walk home?" Chloe asked. "I can order a taxi?"

"I don't mind. Ye, get a taxi, we can all jump in," Louise requested, collecting her things.

Fifteen minutes later the taxi arrived; they all clambered in, laughing and giggling to one another as a result of a full afternoon of drinking.

"I had fun, thanks for having us," Freya spoke as she hugged Chloe.

"See you later," they all said as they shut the door.

Talking amongst themselves, the taxi driver didn't say a word, stopping at each house with Freya's being the last. Each of them handed change to her as they clambered out. Finally arriving home, she handed over the money, thanked him and climbed out of the taxi.

Walking through her gate she spotted a guy-shaped figure sat on her doorstep looking asleep. Feeling alarmed, she panicked. Bravely, she moved slowly towards her front door with her phone in hand ready to ring someone if she needed.

"Hello... Are you alright?" she quizzed worriedly.

"Freya... Freya, I have been waiting for you." He

woke quickly, sounding relieved.

Suddenly feeling sobered up, she shivered as the cold wind blew around her.

"Matt?! Is that you?" She recognised his voice as he spoke, stepping closer to him as her eyes adjusted to the darkness, allowing her to see him more clearly.

"Ye, it's me, I am so sorry to show up like this, I don't know anyone else who lives around here," he slurred.

"Come on, get up," she commanded as she grabbed his arm, pulling him up. "Been drinking, I assume," she interrogated. "How the tables have turned." She laughed at their current situation.

"Well a little, slept it off a bit," he spoke as he walked into her home, adjusting his eyes as Freya turned the lights on.

She eyed him up and down; he was looking sexy dressed in dark navy jeans, Timberland boots and a light grey collared top. He seemed to have grown more facial hair over the summer holidays, making him look more rugged, the look she generally favoured.

"You look freezing, do you want a hot drink?" Freya asked, sounding concerned.

"Thank you, I'll have a coffee please. The weather has taken a bit of a dip in temperature tonight and I didn't bring a jacket, did I? Although I wasn't expecting to be stranded here."

She boiled the kettle. Without hesitation she couldn't help but question how she had gotten into the circumstance of having her hot teacher sat on her doorstep past midnight to then be talking about the weather. She was tired and was hoping to have gone straight bed after she got home.

Directing him into her living room she passed him his drink and sat on the armchair.

"So I have to ask, why are you sat on my sofa this late, in this mess?" she questioned, gazing upon him, waiting for an interesting story.

He sipped his coffee and made himself comfortable on the sofa, giving off a sigh.

"Well it's not much of a story. I was on a date, someone I met online. She seemed alright, and we were having a laugh." He paused.

Freya listened without saying a word; butterflies flew within her stomach making her feel nauseous, caused by the jealousy which rose when he mentioned he was dating, although she now knew he was single.

"We were dancing and I noticed she seemed to be getting drunk quite quickly; she disappeared for while so I went looking for her. I found her outside popping pills." He paused, giving a yawn. "That's not my scene so I left. It wasn't until I left that I remembered I stupidly put my wallet and phone in her bag when we were dancing. I couldn't get a taxi with no money or contact anyone to come and get me, the next minute I'm walking here. I borrowed some guy's phone and emailed you so you might have one from me."

"Oh ye, sorry, I've been out round my friend's all afternoon. I saw it but didn't read it. Damn it, I feel guilty now," she apologised. "I feel privileged you know my email address," she giggled. "Sorry about your date. Make sure you cancel your cards and report your phone," sounding mature.

"I will, once I can get access to them," he smiled.

"Here, you can use my phone, do what you need to do," she spoke as she handed it over willingly. "I hope you don't mind, but I'm shattered I need to go to bed," as she looked at the clock. "You can crash here and I'll drive you home in the morning," she added.

"If you don't mind that would be great. Thank you, it seems the tables have turned," he replied as he laughed, reading her mind.

She passed him pillows and a quilt for the sofa. He sincerely seemed like he felt awful for putting her out, his smile faded like he had really had a shit night and she didn't like seeing him sad. She made her way out of the room, stopping in her tracks, and looked back at him. He was making himself comfy; he caught her gaze.

"If it's any consolation, you are much better than online dating," she smirked. He smiled back, not saying anything. She flicked the light off and went to bed, drifting off quickly, looking forward to seeing him in the morning.

*

7:21am read upon the alarm clock as she opens her eyes. After getting in bed past 2am she feels like she hasn't slept. She rolls over, hugging her pillow with her bare tanned legs tangled within the quilt, trying to get back to sleep. After tossing and turning for ten minutes she gives in, sits up and stretches her body. After consuming bottles of wine all afternoon yesterday her head feels fuzzy and her stomach churns. Skipping down the stairs, she is startled by

Matt standing in her kitchen, who she had completely forgotten about. Realising she's stood in front of him looking a mess in her baggy shorts, an old t-shirt and bed hair, she feels her cheeks flush with embarrassment, although he has already seen her in her worst state.

"Morning Freya." He sounded chirpier, fully dressed and looking fresher having recovered from his evening antics. "I didn't know what you liked so I made some breakfast with what I could find, I hope you don't mind."

She smiled at the choice of breakfast laid upon the counter: boiled eggs, croissants, yoghurt, toast and granola, tea, coffee and fruit juices. Feeling her stomach rumble she was happy to eat anything, although she was fancying a cooked breakfast but did appreciate his efforts.

She took the tea and sat upon the bar stool staring at him as he stared back.

"Thanks Matt, you didn't have to."

She took a croissant and spread it with jam, followed by granola and yoghurt. She fell surprisingly silent, feeling in awe of the situation.

"It's the least I could do for you letting me stay last night," he thanked her. His eyes not moving off of her, tension built within her body as she felt intimidated, wishing she knew what he was thinking.

"Don't worry about it, did you sleep OK?" she asked.

"Ye, I did thanks, although it was short."

"Me too, I can't believe I am awake having only

had five hours' sleep," she yawned.

As they chatted whilst picking at breakfast, she decided Matt didn't judge her based on her appearance and genuinely seemed like a really nice guy. After all these years and trying to look good for him she was sat in raggy clothes with messy hair and he didn't care. The embarrassment she felt soon disappeared as she became more relaxed around him.

"Right, I'll go get showered and take you home?" she planned although he didn't seem in a rush to leave and she also did not want him to go.

"Ye, that's fine with me if you don't mind."

"Not at all, I don't have any plans today anyway."

As she climbed from the stool he stepped towards her; the tension between them could be cut with a knife. She stared upon him once more, unable to read his intentions.

His dark eyes lock onto hers as she finds herself biting her lip. She breathes heavily. If only she could kiss him. She has fancied him for so long she was pining at the idea of touching him. Coming to like him more and more as she grew to know him; her body aches for him and her mind is frazzled at the thought of not knowing how he felt. He stood watching her in anticipation, maybe he feels the same. He steps back, letting out a sigh. She places her cup and bowl down in the sink as his eyes burn into her every move.

"I won't be long," she spoke, breaking the silence as she left the room. "Do whatever, garden's there if you want some fresh air or watch TV, please yourself."

He nodded and watched her walk towards the stairs, watching her ass bounce in her loose shorts. She caught his eye and smirked.

As she walked out of sight she let out a large breath of relief. Unable to control her thoughts she now needed a cold shower more than ever. Feeling horny, she needed to take the edge off before spending time in a compact car with him. As she undressed her body tingled, her mind leading itself astray; if only she could go downstairs now and see how he would react. Her pussy filled with juices as she made her way into the shower. The cold water hit, her making her gasp, her fingers quickly making their way to her soaked pussy as she groped her breasts. Biting her lip feeling naughty for pleasuring herself whilst he sat downstairs waiting.

Becoming lost in the moment within her pleasure, she feels hot and eager to climax. Her fingers circling faster and harder as water runs down her body.

"Can I help?" A manly voice came from the bathroom door, making her jump out of her skin.

"Holy shit!! How embarrassing," she awkwardly exhaled.

Slamming the water off, she grabs her towel and steps out coming face to face with him. Now having the chance she has been waiting for, standing naked and wet before him.

"I'm sorry, I over stepped the boundary quite a bit, but I couldn't stay away any longer." True words fall from Matt's lips as he stands in front of her. She's silent.

His gaze tells her exactly what he wants.

Matt roughly grips the towel wrapped around her, pulling her body close to his, aggressively planting a kiss on her lips. The tension between them is broken within an instant. She groans, entwining his hair within her fingers, dropping the towel. Now stood naked before him, his hands touch her for the first time, sending sparks all over her body. Her body tenses, climaxing at the touch of him. She moans as his lips fall between her teeth, his hands tightly upon her face. She breathes out as he lets go. His eyes wandering all over her, taking her all in, now knowing what he is able to play with. His big, soft hands touch her bare skin making her pine for more, her body tingling all over, feeling her erect nipples rub against his shirt. Unable to believe she is finally going to get to have the man she's wanted for the past three years.

He grabs her hand, taking her to her bed. She unbuckles his belt, letting his jeans fall to the floor as he removes his shirt. She nibbles at his neck as he kisses her shoulder, each impatient to taste each other after all this time. Matt's hand finds her long wet hair whilst the other fumbles on her breast. Pushing him against the bed, he sits naked. She takes control as she straddles his lap whilst they kiss. She's so ready for him, her pussy pulsing at the thought of him inside her; able to feel his erection beneath her, she knows he's ready for her. She eyes up his toned abs as her fingers caress his body, her long nails tickling him, making his body flinch at her gentle touch.

He lifts her up with his strong arms, standing with her nude body wrapped around his waist. He playfully throws her onto the bed. Noticing her eye mask he grabs it off the dresser, placing it over her eyes. Open to playing, she does not refuse. Unable to see, her mind goes into frenzy, goose bumps raise within her skin as her body tingles from head to toe. He's touching her, teasing her as she waits with anticipation of his next move, her body aching for him. She feels his lips near her knees. She inhales. He's breathing heavily as he makes his way up her leg with his warm tongue and gentle kisses.

As he kisses her lower lips she gasps; her hands make their way quickly to his hair – it feels soft as it falls between her fingers. She wants to grab him, caress him, lick him, bite him, kiss him all over and feel his cock inside her, her pussy pounding for him. Fighting the urge to look at him she keeps her hands on him. His wicked tongue caresses her g-spot, making her cum quickly. Her nails dig in his shoulders as she lets out every scream. As her clit becomes sensitive he stops; his hands grope her tits, playing with her large nipples as they are now face to face, unknowing to her.

"Don't stop." She asks for more, panting.

"Of course," he exhales, "I am not finished with you yet," teasing.

His lips lock with hers as her tongue entwines with his. She can taste her sex. He groans, holding her body tightly, the feel of her body against his sends him wild. His penis pulses, shining with precum, he is ready to go. He straddles her as she wraps her legs around him, his cock within her region. As his cock enters her for the first time his thrusts leave her speechless. Her dainty hands caress his back, allowing him to know she likes it. He removes the mask, gazing into her brown eyes. She smiles, biting her lips.

His body responds, pumping into her. As he thrusts hard into her he feels good, plunging in and out, both enjoying every move. Becoming breathless, his erection feeling solid and ready to explode, he is not quite ready yet. He pulls out, allowing her body to relax. He grabs her body, placing her on top of him.

Making it clear it's her turn, she lowers her opening onto his pulsing cock causing her body to shiver. His length hits her g-spot hard causing tingles to spark within her loins. He places his hands on her hips, slowly guiding her as she finds the rhythm between them both. Freya looks down at him as she rides him, where no words are spoken. Embracing the pleasure, his breathing becomes heavy just as her body becomes tired. She knows he's ready. She rides him harder and faster as her body starts to ache. She leans her hands onto his shoulders. His grip tightens around her warm flesh; he moans, "Oh God, fuck me!"

"Oh my god," she joins as she climaxes with him. Her body slows as she catches her breath, eyeing up his erect nipple and his tense abs. He looks flustered. His grip loosens from her body, allowing her to lift off of him and collapse beside him looking full of sex.

He looks at her, catching her smiling. "I've waited three years for that," she laughed.

He laughed, slapping her ass cheek playfully. "Worth the wait I hope," he said.

"Definitely," she smiled.

Rising from the bed she made her way into the bathroom and turned the shower back on. She washed her hair and rinsed the smell of sex off of herself. As the water washed away the bubbles Matt stood within the doorway with his body bare, allowing her to ogle him. She enjoyed what she could see as arousal rose within her pussy once again. Unable to believe she had finally got him where she wanted, she now didn't want him to leave. He opened the shower door and climbed in. She moved aside allowing him to rinse under the water; he stood looking down at her whilst she was lathered in bubbles, his hand reaching round the back of her neck, pulling her in for a kiss. She eagerly responded, they stood close, their bodies pushed up against each other as they kissed, nibbling and groping each other under the falling water. She felt like she was in one of her dreams. As Matt took a breath she rinsed her hair, allowing it to fall long down her back. As he watched he kissed her forehead and climbed out. She felt relaxed as the warm water fell on her skin. She questioned what she was feeling within this very moment, was it lust, was it passion or was she actually growing feelings for him? After all, Chris had not long exited the scene, although she had never felt the way about him the way Matt made her feel.

Feeling clean and refreshed she climbed out and dried herself. Back in her bedroom Matt was unseen; she threw on her red bra and matching French undies, covering them with comfy shorts and a dark green vest top. She quickly towel dried her hair, applied a layer of foundation and a flick of mascara and joined Matt back downstairs who seemed to be cleaning up breakfast.

"Ready to go?" she asked.

"Ye," he spoke, sounding quieter than before.

"You alright?"

"Ye, I'm alright, I would much rather stay and spend the day with you though," he admitted.

Unsure of what to say, Freya just smiled.

He shunned her silence with a smirk and made his way to the front door; she followed.

In a compact car the scent of sex still hung onto his skin. He became her distraction from driving for an hour which she couldn't act on. The image of pulling into a lay-by and fucking him in the back seat of her car crossed her mind numerous times, making her loins ache with desire. She wanted more of him. Breaking the silence, she confessed the nightmare she faced during her physical assessment which he found amusing. In return he openly admitted he had fancied her since she first walked into his classroom. Having to act professional he became tense around her, causing his distant attitude. He also experiencing uncontrollable thoughts as she touched his body that day.

They arrived at his house; he kissed her on the cheek, saying goodbye, and climbed out of the car, leaning down towards her through her window.

"I'll hear from you soon, ye?" he insisted.

"Ye," she reassured, smiling up at him, biting her lip.

CHAPTER 9

Jack

Her drive home passed by quickly as music blared through the speakers, feeling happy with how her weekend had turned out, having finally been able to get to know Matt. Maybe this was the start of something? The intensity caused by not being able to have him had finally been fulfilled, although she now felt more horny knowing he could please her so well, satisfying every ache of her body which she experienced at the thought of him. Matt seemed great inside and out, he had taken a punch for her, looked after her when she was intoxicated, drove her home and been a complete gentleman this whole weekend. The question was, would they see each other again? She hoped so.

Feeling tired after little sleep she slumped herself into the sofa, sighing with relief of a rest. Her eyes feeling heavy, slowly shutting, fighting each blink. She slowly drifted off into a deep sleep for a short time which she was awoken from when she heard her phone ringing from within the kitchen where she had left it on charge. In no rush she climbed off the sofa to get the call, missing it. Removing the charger she scrolled through her notifications to find the call was an unknown number. Shrugging her shoulders she waited to see if a voicemail would be left, when she remembered an unread text message from Jack the night before.

Freya I'm home for the weekend. Can I see you?

Jack

Xxx

Her stomach somersaulted; the thought of Jack being home in walking distance gives her butterflies every time. *Maybe I should see him in person to discuss his letter, strictly as friends. Call it a day?* she thought. Although this upset her, she hated how it had become like this. She knew she would always love him and just wished they could just be friends, however something between them didn't allow it to be so easy. After finally getting with Matt she was hoping she could just want one guy but would her temptations let her? As she and Matt were fresh she didn't feel guilty about seeing Jack. After all it was just as friends. Right?

Hi Jack.

Sorry for the late reply, I am free today, if you're about?

Freya

x

Hi

fancy coming to my mum's birthday meal with me? I know she would love to see you?

xx

This was not really her idea of opportunity to break it off with him but the rumble in her stomach made it difficult to turn down the image of a nice tasty meal. Plus, it would be nice to see his family after all these years.

I could do that ☺

x

Perfect, I'll be there in half hour to pick you up?

x

Ok, thank you

x

She headed up stairs and dressed herself in a vest top, tucking it into a high-waisted skirt, accompanied by a belt and some dolly shoes. Looking trim as ever with her tanned skin on show she felt more comfortable in her own skin than ever before. After quickly straightening her hair and topping up her makeup she was ready to mingle and let Jack see what he was missing out on in the process.

Jack pulled up on her drive way within the half hour. Having known him all these years she failed to ever remember a time where he was late to something. Punctuality must come with the job and with having no patience in waiting around she seemed to favour this about him. She watched his every move through the window; he stepped out of the car looking as handsome as ever, his hair looking a bit longer from the time before as it was slightly gelled. Eyeing him up, his face was sun-kissed with freckles from travelling, dressed in a white buttoned shirt with navy knee-length shorts and new trainers by the looks of how clean they were. She opened the door before he even knocked.

"Hi," she spoke with a beaming smile. He stepped in the doorway and gave her a kiss on the cheek as she inhaled his scent; she really did enjoy the smell of guys probably a bit too much. "You look amazing," he complimented, "summer really does suit you."

"Thank you, not looking too bad yourself," she responded cheerfully. She locked the door as Jack made his way to the car, the door open ready for her to get in.

"You do move on fast, don't you!" she heard from the path. Turning her head to face the direction of the voice she stared upon Chris. "What are you doing here?" she hissed, feeling angry at the sight of him, hating how fired up he made her feel as he stood before her with his bulging biceps and pecs on show. She tried not to look.

She stopped in her tracks and walked towards him, with Jack looking on from the driver's seat, his face frowning with confusion. "I'm allowed to run aren't

I?" he sneered.

"Chris, I told you to stay away from me, it means don't come running past my house to see what I'm doing!" she viciously spoke.

Jack climbed out of the car, slamming the door as he noticed Freya's mood change. "Oi, what's going on? Who the fuck are you?" he bluntly questioned. His body stood tense with his arms crossed beside her.

"Jack it's fine, ignore him, he's just being a prick," she insisted.

"She's a slut, I hope you know what you're getting yourself into!" Chris bellowed, loud enough for oncomers to hear, completely embarrassing her as she looked around.

"What the hell, Chris? I did nothing to deserve this abuse, you seriously have major issues!" she cried with anger, hating the fact Jack was witnessing this.

"That's enough, I don't know who you are or whatever this is but you're out of order, you don't speak to a lady like that, especially Freya, in front of me." Jack's body stood on edge like any military guy would do in a confrontation, looking ready to charge.

"Well you aren't the guy she was with this morning, so she can't prove me wrong," he spoke, looking down at her, making her feel ashamed. *Oh God, that makes me sound great,* she thinks.

"Are you stalking me or something?" she questioned, confused as to how he knew what she was doing this morning.

Chris stepped onto her driveway, making her feel intimidated as he towered above her, also being a few inches taller than Jack.

"Where is Matt now? Gone home for a change of clothes? Does he know about this one?" he snarled, looking back and forth towards Jack, shaking his head.

"That's it, I've had enough," Jack snapped, placing a fist into Chris's face, throwing him backwards with a daze. Startled, he came back at Jack full force with his body weight whacking him back with a thud, knocking him aside. Punches being thrown back and forwards with neither of them backing down. Freya yelling at them to stop. Neighbours and passers-by began to stop to see what was going on. Unaware of Jack's background Chris didn't expect to be losing comparing his body size to Jack's. He looked dumbfounded, trying his hardest to knock Jack off his feet. Freya, unable to stop the scuffle was crying with anger and concern for Jack, his white shirt now covered in blood.

"Jack, please stop!" she begged.

Chris hit the floor with a thud from Jack's last swing, his face covered in cuts and swollen bruises. Both looked as bad as each other. Grabbing Jack by the hand she takes him back to his car where he sits upon the bonnet, Freya checking he's OK. An onlooker helped Chris to his feet as a police car pulled up. Two policemen and a policewoman climbed out, one addressing Chris, the other making their way to Jack, and another asking witnesses before questioning Freya.

In complete shock about what had just happened, this now being the second time Chris's fists had been involved, she was unable to control her tears. *What a complete turn of events,* she thought.

"It's my fault, not Jack's. Chris is an ex, he's become jealous and by the sounds of it has been stalking me as he said he was here this morning too," she continued as the officer took notes. "It's also not the first fight he's been in, he punched my university lecturer a few days ago. Jack was just defending me just now, that's all," she explained looking over at him.

He gazed back at her, with a look in his eye like he wished he had not bothered to stop by. Her heart beating hard within her chest, she felt sick and just wanted to make sure he was OK and apologise for ruining his weekend home.

After giving her statement she made her way back to Jack after being reassured Chris was being given a restraining order; she felt relieved. Chris was removed from sight; he didn't say anything to anybody. As she walked towards Jack she overheard the police officer.

"Jack, with your job background you could have caused serious harm, this will not look good on your record and you will face serious consequences, especially as you started the fight." Hearing his career could be in jeopardy over her stupid choice in men she felt nothing but pure guilt, leaving her questioning her current behaviour when it came to men. She really had done it this time.

Freya opened her front door to get Jack some ice for his swollen fists and face. Silence filled the room as he removed his bloody shirt, rinsing away the blood from his face and knuckles.

"Jack, I am so sorry," she quietly spoke, feeling

unsure of how he currently felt. "I don't know what you're thinking but I'm hoping the truth is not as bad as you're making out in your head. I don't just go from man to man and I hope you don't think I'm some kind of slut. I would hate for you to think that of me," she cried, unable to control her emotion. Jack stood silent with a split lip swelling up as the ice brought out the bruise. He winced at the pain.

"Freya, what you do is your business, not mine, and I would never think you're a slut." He was unable to express without pain running through his face. "Although it does sound like you have quite a story when it comes to men, I do have to say, but like I said it's not my concern." He paused. "Not anymore anyway." His words stung as the truth left his lips.

"Come on, I'm already really late, I need to get a new shirt, not that I don't look a mess anyway," he murmured.

"You sure you still want me to come? I understand if you want me to stay here," she asked, unsure whether she wanted to explain the look of her son to his mother on her birthday.

"You're coming, end of." He ushered her out of the front door for the second time.

"What will happen to you back at work?" she questioned on the ride over.

"That I don't know, hopefully it will just be a fine, it all depends if he presses charges," sounding concerned about returning to work on Monday. "Just forget about it, it's not your fault. Whatever happens you didn't tell me to punch him, that was my choice. Maybe I need to control my emotions when I'm around you and not be so protective, especially as it's not my place," he admitted, glancing over as her spoke.

"Maybe." She failed to respond with much more, feeling awful.

They pulled onto his mum's large gravelled drive; balloons and banners were seen along the fence. Music was heard and BBQ food could be smelt within the summer's air.

"I thought you said dinner?" she questioned, climbing out of the car.

"Well a BBQ is dinner, it's a garden party," he clarified.

"Oh nice, at least you don't have to go into a fancy restaurant looking like that," she giggled, trying to clear the tension, looking at his swollen blooded face.

Freya suddenly felt nervous about entering Jack's childhood home, the house she spent many years in. She followed him through the front door, observing him being welcomed by friends and family. They stood observing his messed up face, a bloody shirt and his chiselled chest and abs completely on show. He didn't seem to be too bothered by it just yet.

"Jack! What the hell happened to you? And for goodness' sake put a top on! You were supposed to be here ages ago!" his mother yelled at him as she made her way through the hall once she spotted him. As she drew closer, noticing his face her concern grew. She was just as mothering as she always had been when he was a young boy which made Freya chuckle as she watched.

"Trying to keep calm, she breathed heavily,

questioning what happened. Jack didn't elaborate.

"I'm fine, just a little scuffle defending Freya," he spoke as he nodded his head towards her.

"Oh, hi Freya, what a long time it's been. You're looking very well," she spoke as she gave her a hug.

"Thank you, it's nice to see you too, happy birthday," she spoke, returning the hug.

"I'm just going to grab a new shirt. Have this, it's probably ruined now though," he spoke as he threw his ruined shirt to his mum, as he took for the stairs.

She observed his home; it smelt exactly the same, it felt the same and it looked the same with all the same family photos on the wall, his school photos hung to be seen which she saw herself within made her smile as she held back her emotion whilst tears tried to fill her eyes.

"Hey Freya, here you go," his mum spoke, handing her a glass of Pimm's. "There are people you might know outside if you want to go through and help yourself to food, I'm sure he will be down in a minute." She smiled, being as friendly as always, even if she had caused her son to look like a complete brute within half hour of being with him.

"Oh and Freya," she heard again as she was about to exit the room, "Jack is thrilled you're here. He's been telling me all weekend he was going to invite you, I really hope you can get over this long-distance stuff and get together." She sounded hopeful.

"Maybe." Freya sipped her drink, smiled and made her way into the garden.

Overlooking the busy garden filled with familiar

faces, family and friends she had met when they were younger, the BBQ was grilling away whilst drinks were being dished out, old-school music was heard playing in the background, drowning out everyone's conversations, and the atmosphere was lively. She walked towards Jack's friends who she spotted in the corner, smiling at them as she said hello to everyone who recognised her.

"Freya Bell, what a surprise to see you here," Ryan said. "Long time no see, you look good, you haven't aged a bit," he complimented her.

"Thank you, you too," she replied.

"Where is Jack?" he queried.

"I'm here," he added as he crept up behind her. She turned, looking over her shoulder, wincing as she looked upon his battered face which seemed to be getting worse as time went by.

"Holy shit! What the hell happened to you?" Dan exclaimed.

"Ha, you should see the other guy!" he bragged as he sipped his Pepsi.

"Really? What happened?" Ryan asked, each of them all eyes on Jack waiting for a story. He caught Freya looking down, still feeling bad about it.

"It's nothing, some guy insulted Freya, it pissed me off, I punched him, and he hit me back," he spoke, trying to limit the details.

Freya bit on her straw, looking up, and smiled at him, thanking him for the lack of details in hope to save her reputation from people she went to school with, although she was sure he would elaborate when she wasn't around.

"Did you win?" Dan laughed.

"What do you think?" he asked.

"Well looking at you, I'm not so sure." They all laughed at the state of him.

The party went on for hours. Freya was enjoying the food, although since she was feeling in an emotional mood she decided not to drink anything other than her first glass of Pimm's. She mingled with old faces, enjoyed catching up with the past and watched Jack relaxing like she used to see. She adored watching him smile and laugh; having always found his laugh infectious, it made her beam without realising. As the evening rolled in, the warmth disappeared and the garden cleared, Freya, Jack and his mates surrounded a large fire flickering away whilst they roasted marshmallows and laughed amongst each other, most of them now pissed and sprightly.

She sat wrapped in one of Jack's hoodies sank into a camping chair. Feeling tired, she could happily fall asleep under the night sky as she was kept warm by the flames. Feeling her eyes drawing closed as she relaxed she was feeling warm and cosy as she listened to everyone talk as she fell silent. Unsure of what time it was she felt her body being lifted by Jack off the chair into his arms like a sleeping toddler. "Come on you, let's go inside."

She went to get down but he held her tightly as he locked the back door. The house was silent as everyone was gone. She stayed within his arms knowing he was strong enough to hold her weight; she felt safe in his arms.

He carried her upstairs and into his old bedroom where they shared plenty of memories. It smelt the same, amazing just like him. Lifting her down onto his bed he pulled the duvet over her and went to walk away.

"Stay here," she asked in a sleepy daze.

He said nothing as he walked towards her; he lifted the covers and climbed over her, lying beside her on his back. The tension between them was as strong as ever, just as it had always been. She turned around, facing him, placing her head on his chest, her arm over his body and her leg between his knees just like they used to cuddle. His arm moved in on her, holding her tightly as she lay there in his hoodie smelling of bonfire. Looking up at the ceiling, he smiled as he closed his eyes.

"I love these cuddles," she spoke as she drifted to sleep.

The grip of Jack's cuddle tightened as she was drifting in and out of sleep throughout the night. The guilt of being with him emerged within her mind as she didn't know where she and Matt stood; she felt just like Chris described her having been in a bed with two different men in the same day. What was she doing? Her mind played havoc on her as she tried to get back to sleep.

Morning soon crept round. Feeling hot when she woke she wished to move but didn't want to wake him. She moved around trying to cool down, placing her legs out of the covers. Laying there uncomfortable for what seemed forever she felt claustrophobic; she pulled her arms into her hoodie, slowly lifting it o her head, trying to keep as still as possible, unaware of how early it was. Throwing the jumper off the bed Jack started to shuffle around. His hands on her body, something she enjoyed very much.

Unable to get back to sleep; the memories filled her mind as she lay within the bed she lost her virginity in some years ago. She gazed around the room in which she spent her teen years. It hadn't changed a bit. The smell, the feel, the sounds outside, all exactly the same, all but Jack. He was now a full grown, mature army soldier, more handsome than ever, yet he still loved her and wanted her more than anything just as before. As she turned to look at him she wanted to stroke his bruised face and cut lip; she felt herself smiling at him, as if he was a new-born baby fast asleep. Confused as to what she was feeling for Jack, she was eager to move so the butterflies in her stomach would stop. Peering at the ceiling, she felt him move, he lifted his head to look at her with a sleepy look. His greys glistened in the sunshine within his brunette hair, his bright blue eyes looking directly at her, making her feel uneasy as silence fell between them. Edging forwards he placed a kiss on her lips. Stunned, she pulled away. Questioning her actions, her feelings for Jack, for Matt, all she felt was confused.

Her body on the other hand did not feel the same, she kisses him back and she tastes him. She loves his flavour. As they kiss their tongues entwine, her hands on his body pulling him in closer. His hands caressing her body over her clothes, tugging at them, wanting hot body. Freya wants him now; her hand orts, wrapping around his large

148

rippled cock. She knows he wants her too. He pulls up her skirt, touching her, slowing caressing her clit, making her body pine for him. Her hands are moving his shaft up and down, his dick feeling as hard as ever. He's breathing fast, his touch unable to concentrate on her. Moving his hand she kisses him, kissing his neck, kissing his shoulder, moving down to his welcoming hard on. Placing it in her mouth she could already taste his precum; his morning glory is solid. Her hands cup his balls, stroking them as her tongue takes control, nibbling on him playfully.

"Oh fuck," he gasped as she tasted his juices filling her mouth.

"Sorry, sorry, sorry," he laughed.

She swallows the tang of him and lets go, licking her lips, letting out a giggle.

"What????" she blushes.

"I wanted you so badly, I have done for ages, and as soon as your tongue touched me I lost control, it..." He hesitated, embarrassed. "Come here," he ordered, pulling on her.

He pulled down her skirt, throwing it on the floor, also stripping her of her pink, lacy thong. Lying on his back he guided her over his body until she was sitting on his face. He kissed her lower lips making her inhale, he took her in his mouth, knowing exactly what to do. She groaned, she moaned. As her orgasm built she didn't want the feeling within her body to stop, her hands up and down the wall trying to control her sounds. She breathed heavier, making him aware she was near to climax. Pulling her hips closer she was as close as she could be; his tongue worked its magic deep within her. Her body released, she cried out a moan as her orgasm shot through her body.

Her body tingled from head to toe as she exhaled. Lifting herself from above him she sat beside him as a sudden feeling ran through her mind. Putting aside how much she cared for him and how satisfied she felt right now she promised herself this time with Jack was just as friends, what about Matt? *I'm such a bitch.* She felt angry at herself.

Climbing off the bed, her mood had now made a quick turn. She found her clothes and put them back on as Jack watched her, unaware of her thoughts.

"What's wrong?" Jack asked as he sat up, leaning against the wall. She hesitated, looking into his concerned eyes. "Freya?" She sat on the edge of the bed once she was dressed and let the words fall out.

"This was great, the party, last night, just now, all great," she recalled.

"I'm not getting that feeling," he spoke as he looked upon her.

"I think this was the perfect way to say goodbye," she choked, fighting back tears.

Jack leant forward, looking confused. "What do you mean? I thought we had fun last night, like old times," he questioned.

"We did, but that's just it, the feelings all come back when we're together but you know why we're not together anymore and that is not going to change... I'm not asking you to change, I don't want you to, but this hurts too much, Jack, knowing I'm going to have to say goodbye again," she continued as tears rolled down her face.

"So you're saying you have feelings for me, but rather than us be great together like you know we would be you want to spend time with twats who treat you like shit." He stood tense, looking down at her.

"No, I'm not saying that." Tension built between them as Jack grew angrier.

"But you are, Freya. I get it, you enjoy being free but maybe you need to grow up," he told her, his voice raising.

"What's that supposed to mean?" she snapped, standing opposite him.

"Well since I last saw you at the beginning of summer what have you done? Ye, you have graduated but now what?" He hesitated. "Have you even applied for jobs? You've obviously had a few guys on the go and look where that's got you." He paused trying his hardest not to say something he would regret as her expression changed; he full well knowing he was upsetting her.

"Freya I think you should go, clearly I'm not worth anything to you, not anything. It's clear to me I am just another guy you fuck when you feel like it! I back you up against some prick shouting at you in the street and get battered for you!" shouting as he stared at her in silence.

"I got arrested, Freya! My job is now on the line and you still can't put aside the distance issue. No matter what I do it's not good enough for you!"

She stood there watching his every move, tears streaming down her face as her lip quivered, unable to talk, her arms crossed over her body, listening, knowing he was completely right.

"I don't know what else I can do for you. After all these years I still love you, I'm still in love with you, I never even fell out of love with you! But you're right, it hurts too much when you don't get the same feelings back," he admitted now sounding completely heartbroken having said it out loud.

"Just go, Freya," he told her as he hit his face in his hands.

"Jack," she spoke, stepping towards him.

"No, Freya, just go," he ordered.

She looked up at his face, seeing the anger and upset within his eyes and his shaking body as he spoke. She fell silent, not knowing what to do or say. Opening the door she looked back at him. Jack was sat with his back against her; she left the room, headed downstairs and straight out of the front door to find herself stepping out into the first rainfall of the summer.

CHAPTER 10

Home Truths

It's cold outside, the rain falls around her, filling her shoes as she slowly walks home, feeling upset and heartbroken all over again. Her eyes hurt from so much crying although it doesn't feel like she will stop anytime soon. This time she blames herself entirely for the mess she is in. She knows Jack is right, for the first time she had her eyes open allowing her to see clearly, seeing how she had become preoccupied in hooking up with guys she hardly knew, drinking too much and lounging around the garden. Not one interview was lined up let alone had she even once opened her laptop to search for a job. She seemed to have forgotten she needed to focus on a career rather than just running the hours away, her marathon also coming up soon. With time now against her as September drew closer she needed to snap out of this summer behaviour.

Having heard the hurtful truth from the one guy she had ever loved, she knew things had to change, she needed to stop spending her savings, start a career, stop behaving like a teenage slut and grow up.

Feeling like she needed to talk it off she took her phone out numerous times, wanting to text Jack. She knew she shouldn't she was doubtful that she would ever hear from him again. She tried to text the girls but didn't know what to write; after all, she knew what they would all say, especially after they had been trying to get her to see sense for weeks about her current behaviour. Wiping the rain off her phone screen, she locked it and put it back into her pocket. The jacket pocket she now seemed to have claimed from Jack.

The tears flowed down her cheeks adding to the rain covering her, her makeup now running completely clear and her hair dripping as is stuck to her face – she was completely soaked. The rain poured, clearing the humidity from the summer air. As she walked she found herself ending up walking into the bar she previously worked at. For what reason she did not know. A friendly face, perhaps.

The door swung shut behind her as the noise echoed within the empty room.

"Freya?" she heard within the dull room. No light was shining through the small windows yet and the lamps were just warming up, it was only 9:30am after all. She spotted Bradley leaning against the bar.

"Bradley? What are you doing here?" she queried as she found her voice, observing him sat with a laptop before him whilst sipping a coffee, the scent filling the room.

"Hey stranger," he spoke as she walked towards the bar. "Are you alright?" he asked, concerned. "What are you doing out in the rain?" he questioned.

"You're soaked, do you want a hot drink and a towel?" he offered.

"Yes please." She shivered, wiping her forehead with Jack's soaking wet hoody sleeves. "Why are you here? It looks like you're working," she quizzed.

"I am, I offered to stay upstairs and work whilst the boss man is on holiday," he explained.

The bar looked left from the night before. Bradley had the morning set-up, a shift she used to hate getting, having to wait around for the first customer, which in this rain would be in a few hours yet. Bradley used to chat to her on her morning shifts when he didn't have many jobs, so she was sure he was glad she was repaying the favour, knowing how boring it is.

He popped out the back whilst her drink brewed; she stood facing the mirror looking up at the state she was. For some reason she never really cared about how she looked around Bradley, over the years he had become more of a friend with benefits rather than a guy she had to impress.

He reappeared, walking round the front of the bar, making his way towards her. He spontaneously gave her a hug despite getting his own clothes wet.

"You look a mess, what's happened?" He put the towel on her shoulders and dabbed her dry. She took it from him as he walked back behind the bar. As he made her drink she stood letting her tears fall, unable to control her emotions.

"Oh, I'm a mess, Bradley. It's finally come to my attention I have completely wasted this summer. I'm in my late twenties with no job, I haven't even looked for one. All I've done in the past few weeks is drink too much, sunbathe all day, run the hours away and hook up with guys." She paused, sipping her tea. "I know I said this summer was to relax but I seem to have relaxed a little too much and now it's nearly over and I have nothing to show for it other than a sun tan, an ex with a restraining order and I've probably lost someone I really care about over my stupid choices," she vented. With no pause she continued until she had finished.

"Calm down, Freya, it really doesn't sound as bad as you think. First maybe have a break from the guys in your life and maybe try to get it down to just one guy? Or none, I don't like hearing about them anyway." He grinned, trying to cheer her up.

"Go home, stick your laptop on and get searching for some jobs. With your skills and experience you shouldn't have a problem, I'm pretty sure you will have interviews lined up next week and go to your marathon and run it, you're going to smash it anyway, and use all them hours to clear your mind," he said, sounding so put together. "How does that sound?" he asked.

"Is it really that easy? I've probably gained myself a reputation of being a right slut, maybe I should hide away for a while. I don't even know how it happened after the last three years of no guys and focusing on my course work. I just came to a point where I just wanted to let go," she muttered.

"Ye, you probably did, just a bit too much too soon, sweetie," he said, wiping her tears. "Stick to one guy, or no guys, you don't need a handful to keep you entertained," he spoke. Considering he was one of the guys he wasn't judging her or questioning her.

"You're right," she admitted.

"I know I am," he joked. "Freya, you're a good-looking girl, you're funny, clever and anyone would be lucky to be with you. I should know, we have had good times," he confessed.

She smiled, pausing as she drank her tea, warming her up from the chill she had gained from the rain.

As he continued to work she sat and watched; she made a plan to finish her summer on a high. To go home and get her ass into gear. "I'm going to head off, Bradley, I'll see you soon," she spoke as he looked over and heard her voice whilst he wiped down tables.

"OK, honey, I'll see you soon!" he shouted over to her and smiled.

She grabbed her bag and headed for the door, the rain having now stopped. Fighting the urge to text Jack to check if he was OK she stopped herself once more. After all, he had not contacted her.

CHAPTER 11

Revelation

After a wet walk home she changed into some warm joggers and a jumper for the first time this summer, warming her up. After tidying her house she sat staring at a blank TV screen trying to decide what to do. The house seemed empty following an evening being surrounded by people. It was quiet and dull. Light shone through the window following the rainstorm; everything seemed quite bleak right now. Through the silence her mind played back and forth on Matt and Jack. Feeling tired of her feelings she tried to get them out of her head but nothing was working.

She stood from her sofa, made her way into the kitchen and boiled the kettle. After grabbing a cuppa and a few biscuits she sat at her table and turned on her laptop for the first time since she had left university. She typed 'Sports Jobs' into the Google search engine and searched for hours until she felt she had exhausted every option and website. A few jobs she had come across took her fancy which she sent her updated CV to, as well as sending in application form after application form to several companies, losing count of how many she had applied for. If it was sports-related, full-time and near enough local, she applied for it. Having gained qualifications in sports, personal training, nutrition and rehabilitation she had plenty of experience and choices to choose from and was not entirely sure which area of the industry she wanted to use. As a child she always fancied being a physical education teacher, although she would need to further her qualifications into teaching for another year. This, she also searched. She jotted down notes about each application and the teaching course information before closing her laptop for the night. Her laptop pinged – an email from Mr M Jones.

Hi Freya

I hope you're alright, thank you for letting me crash at yours the other night, sorry for putting you out. I really appreciate it. I must say I thoroughly enjoyed your company, it's been nice getting to know you now I can. I hope to see you again soon?

Matt

She read the email, smiling at his words, feeling her heart skip a beat, knowing she fancied him. A schoolgirl crush fluttered within her body at the very thought of him. Although she wanted to see him she did feel like she needed some time off men after being reminded of her behaviour by Jack. Although she did want to be honest with him in case something ever did happen between them. After much thought into finding the right words she emailed him back to clear her guilty conscience.

Hi Matt

You're welcome, I'm glad I was able to help, it was great to see you too. I really enjoyed our time together. I would love to see you again although I feel right now may not be the best time. In all honesty after you left I encountered another run in with Chris. Long story short it turns out he has been watching my house, he saw you leave and an old school friend Jack come and pick me up a few hours later to take me to his mums birthday party. It's not what it sounds like, I'm hoping you don't jump the gun although we did kiss, but I regretted it instantly as I really like you and there is nothing between us, not anymore.

Anyway I am going to spend the next few weeks applying for jobs and attending interviews (hopefully) in hope to get a move on with a career plan, plus I have my marathon training.

I hope I haven't put you off seeing me again. Keep in touch.

Freya

She shut her laptop, feeling much better than she did when she had first sat down. Having released her guilt and made progress on career choices she felt a weight had been lifted from her shoulders. The argument with Jack really had seemed to allow her to see more clearly. Although she so badly wanted to text him to tell him she knew it was not the right choice.

Her phone rang as it sat in her hand, making her heart sink. She glanced at the screen hoping it was Jack, it was Louise.

"Hey Lou, you alright?"

"Ye I'm alright. My day didn't start so great but it's got better, but I'll explain when I see you."

"Ye, I'll be at the engagement party tomorrow." Freya planted a head slap across her forehead as she had forgotten about it.

"See you tomorrow."

"Love you, bye."

As the night drew in she found herself watching crappy TV, eating more comfort food; she really needed to get back on her healthy eating regime before the weight started piling on. Her eyes felt heavy as the screen flashed in the darkness, causing her to drift. She shut the TV off and went to bed early for once.

After the first good night in a while she woke to another morning of heavy rain hammering against the window. She decided to ditch the run she had planned for the second time this week, much to her dismay as her marathon was creeping round fast. Although some tapering within her training maybe beneficial, she thought. Instead she chose to have a major sort out through her clothes in order to see whether she had anything suitable for interviews. She filled charity bags with clothes and shoes she didn't wear anymore. Feeling productive with her day, she was looking forward to a stress-free night with her friends.

She grabbed her Mac, hitting the on button, letting it load whilst she ran herself a bubble bath. Having mooched through her outfits which she had placed aside she had a few choices for the party; some of her old favourites were hanging amongst her clothes rail which she had come across having been hidden at the back of the wardrobe. Her email box pinged after ping, making her feel excitedly nervous. Opening her emails she scanned through the inbox, coming across several replies from her job applications. Noticing a few companies she preferred she read those first, each thanking her for her application, asking for availability for interviews. She exhaled a deep breath, smiling, feeling proud of herself, relieved that on paper she had potential. Being offered several sport managerial roles, sports therapy roles and an exercise GP referral role available to her, she had a tough decision to make and needed to choose where she really wanted to end up. She sat perched on the toilet seat watching the bubbles rise, typing away replying to each offer, her next week's calendar now full of interviews. Trying not to think too much about how nervous interviews made her, she opened Matt's reply which by looking at it he had responded to straight away. Not knowing what he would now think of her she became anxious as she read the words slowly.

Hi Freya

Are you free next week? I have managed to get you an interview for a job within the university if you fancy it? Working within the sports department as long as you can do your teaching alongside it which we can discuss? You would be perfect for the job. Wednesday at 10.00am in campus? Let me know.

Matt

His message leaving her feeling dumbfounded, her mind boggled, not knowing what to think.

First he had completely ignored her honesty which left her questioning where they stood with each other. On another note his offer sounded perfect, it was a dream job – teaching her passionate subject, summers off, working with people she already knew within a great university campus, she felt she had been given an opportunity she couldn't turn down. Although she couldn't help but think Matt had pulled a few strings and maybe the fact she had slept with him had something to do with it? Now she didn't know what to do…

Hi Matt…

She typed, taking a deep breath as she hesitated at what to say. She shut her laptop, putting it aside, and undressed herself for a soak in the bath where she relaxed, thinking about her choices. Was working with Matt really a sensible move? What if it didn't work out between them? How awkward would that be? She mulled over her current options, a few being long hours all year round and some she wasn't so keen on, a full-time teaching job seemed like a perfect fit for her lifestyle. Becoming annoyed at herself for even thinking about turning the interview opportunity down she shunned the idea of saying no. *Of course I'm going,* she thought to herself.

Following a soak where she thoroughly exfoliated her skin and treated her hair and face to a mask she felt as refreshed as ever. She sat in her towel at her dresser to dry and straighten her hair. Noticing it took a lot longer than normal, she messaged her hairdresser, asking for an appointment for a colour and a cut as it had been a while. With the sun being on it and it constantly being put up, it didn't feel in the best condition, like it normally was. Another appointment jotted into her diary for next week which was now looking pretty full.

She applied a little make-up and threw on an off-the-shoulder, flowery, flowy dress. Her tan looking as good as ever from head to toe, it really had been a hot summer this year. As she went to leave she sat on her chair, re-opening her laptop whilst she pulled on her black wedge sandals. Buckling them up, she was now ready to go when Chloe arrived as arranged. Clicking back onto her emails, she continued to type.

Hi Matt

Thank you so much for the interview opportunity within the university, this sounds like a dream job. I am definitely free.

Thank you again

Freya

She decided to take off the '*xx*'. Smiling, she shut her laptop, happy with her decision, feeling proud of not obsessing over why he failed to respond to her email. Choosing not to dwell on it, she stayed optimistic for her upcoming busy week next, an engagement party tonight was the perfect way to end her day and relax. As she strutted down the stairs she eyed herself up in the onlooking mirror where her reflection made her feel confident. Chloe walked in. "Hey Chloe."

"Hi," she responded as she gave her a hug.

"Thanks for picking me up," Freya said.

"No problem, I'm not drinking anyway so feel free to enjoy some bubbly."

Grabbing Nina's gift off the unit, they complimented each other's outfits as they left the house.

On the journey over to Nina's large house they caught up. Freya went on about all her drama with Jack, her gossip with hot Matt and her nightmares with Chris. To her surprise Chloe didn't have a lot to say, she probably didn't know what to say. Although it felt good to let it out and admit her problems to herself and Chloe. As she heard herself talk her recent behaviour did sound like a TV drama which made her realise how reckless she had been all summer. She felt ashamed of her behaviour. In hope of starting fresh, she pushed her current feelings for herself aside, planning to enjoy some time with her girlfriends.

As they made their way to Nina's, there were cars among cars surrounding the house. They had begun to overflow the street which was becoming busy. Chloe drove around looking for a place to park as party guests were seen making their way towards to the house.

"I have a feeling this is going to be a big party," Freya laughed as she looked at Chloe.

"Ye, me too," Chloe giggled.

Finally parking what seemed five minutes' walk away, they made their way into the house which looked like it had been professionally decorated with silver, gold and white balloons. There were engagement banners hanging on the walls, large bouquets of flowers were seen within the rooms and large stacks of *Prosecco* glasses piled perfectly for the hundreds of guests which were all about her house.

"Nina, congratulations to you and Ben again, you really do know how to through a proper party, I didn't know you knew this many people," Freya laughed as she cuddled her and kissed her cheek.

"Thanks, Frey. You look gorgeous, you look really well, and look at your tan!" she complimented. "Pretty much all our family and friends are here. Ben has a large family and many friends. There are also a few business associates here. We just thought let's invite everyone and have a real party," she boasted. Nina stood before them in a long silver dress; she looked gorgeous with her red hair flowing down to her thin waist. She looked a million dollars even without the huge house and hired waiters showing her fortune. Freya was in a perfectly good mood which for once left her feeling no ounce of jealously over Nina's career success, or her engagement to her childhood sweetheart. She was 100% happy for her.

As Freya mooched around the room saying hello to Nina's guests she sipped on *Prosecco* and enjoyed the canapés being passed around. She and Chloe were enjoying the eye candy as there were numerous good-looking suited and booted men before them.

"How about that one?" Chloe pointed. A handsome, brunette, grey-suited man stood across the room. "Umm, well he is good looking, I'm saying he's around 35, he definitely looks rich, I would say he's probably an accountant or lawyer, but he's definitely not single," Freya giggled.

"Ye, you're right. Ah, how depressing, we're nearly middle aged and single. I would love a sparkly ring on my finger, planning a wedding," Chloe moped as Freya felt their fun game had suddenly took a turn into reality of their single lives.

"Chloe, what! You have everything, you could have any of these guys in this room, at least you have your shit together. I on the other hand really don't," Freya confessed.

"True," she smiled.

"Oi!" Freya elbowed her, laughing as they both sat people watching.

"How about him at 12 o'clock, just walked into the room, he's hot. God, his arms are massive." Chloe gawked. "He's definitely not single"

Freya looked around to spot the guy in question, dropping her glass on the carpet.

"Oh shit." A waiter quickly came over to clean the mess up, handing her another drink. "I'm so, so sorry," she spoke as she moved aside, letting the waiter by. "Thank you," she said as she took her drink, quickly swigging at it.

She continued to scan the room. A sudden feeling of nausea hit her stomach as she saw him.

"Oh no, Chloe he is definitely single! I have to go." Freya stood up quickly.

"Wait what's wrong?" Chloe asked, concerned, standing up next to her, looking over at him. "That's Chris!" What the fuck is he doing here?" she cried out. "Is that Louise he's with?!" They observed her walk in the room next to him, dressed in a beautiful red dress showing off all her curves with a huge smile upon her face.

"She looks really good," Chloe said to Freya.

"Ye, she does, I need to talk to her." Freya stormed off in her direction, Chris noticing her straight away with a grin on his face, rolling his eyes as they followed her out of the room.

"Louise, I need to speak to you." She grabbed her arm and led her into the entrance hall.

"Err, hi Freya, Chloe, what's going on?!" Louise questioned.

"Why are you here with him?" Freya bellowed.

"Chris? He is my plus one," she snapped as she gazed upon him through the doorway. "What the hell, Freya?" Louise spoke, confused.

"He has to leave! I don't want him near me." Freya raised her voice.

"Freya, calm down," Chloe quietly spoke.

"No, he doesn't need to leave! Just because you're not dating doesn't mean he isn't allowed near you." she spoke.

"OH, she doesn't know?" Chloe butted in.

Chris strolled into the hall with a creepy smirk on his face, looking proud of his accomplishment. Yet again he had ruined Freya's day just by walking into a room.

"I don't know what?" Louise asked, looking at Freya, then back at Chris.

"Oh ye, sorry babe, I didn't tell you, I'm not allowed near Freya, I have a restraining order," he explained calmly, acting like it was no issue as he looked evilly into Freya's eyes.

"Why? What's happened?" Louise looked confused. "Why didn't you say something when you knew she would be here? I'm so confused right now!" Louise continued, becoming agitated. She stood with her arms crossed, her heel started to tap against the wooden flooring whilst she waited for answers.

Freya stood feeling guilty for ruining her moment; as she saw Louise's smile disappear she went to explain. "Oh, does it really matter!" he butted in. "All I have to do is walk in the room and it rattles her cage every time! Isn't that right, Freya!" he spoke, getting in her face.

"Don't come near me, you bastard," Freya snapped, stepping back as a few onlookers turned towards them.

"Chris," Louise pulled him back to her side by his hand, "can you leave please?" Louise spoke towards him with her hands firmly on his chest as if to control him.

"Babe?" he responded with puppy-dog eyes. "No, Chris, just leave, I'll see you tomorrow, ye?" she sternly spoke towards him.

He looked at her, glancing to Freya then back at her. He kissed her on the cheek and walked out as Louise watched him.

"I'm sorry Louise, I should have told you. Well I would have if I knew you were dating him," Freya explained, her tone now soft with guilt for ruining her date.

"Freya, this isn't the place, we can catch up on that another time," Louise quickly silenced her, changing the topic.

"We definitely need to catch up more often, seems we're all missing juicy details," Chloe laughed, trying to change the mood.

"Definitely," they all said, laughing amongst each other. "Louise, you look amazing by the way!" Chloe nudged her.

"Sexy as," Freya added hoping she wasn't angry with her.

"Thanks, I have been working hard these past few weeks, I've lost a stone," she added, smiling, showing off her new waist line.

"Well done!" Chloe added.

Walking back into the busy room, the clinging of glasses were heard. The talking stopped and everyone had eyes on Nina and her new fiancé, Ben, a well-mannered, friendly, tall, blond, clean-shaved, slim guy who made his fortune through business and inheritance.

"Hi everyone," he spoke with his hand wrapped around Nina, with the biggest smile on both of their faces. "We would like to thank you all for joining us to celebrate our engagement. Standing here stood next to my beautiful fiancée in front of all you very special people makes me the luckiest man in the world. We appreciate all your love, kind words, and lovely gifts. We look forward to celebrating our perfect day with all of our friends and family.

"I'm sure as far as the planning the wedding goes, I will not understand the importance of themes, flowers and dresses, although I am sure with my best men, the bridesmaids, parents and many of you here we will get through the disputes together," he laughed.

"I cannot wait till the day I get to call Nina my wife. I love you, baby, thank you for being you," he finished, staring into her eyes before planting a kiss on her lips.

Everyone clapped and cheered to the happy couple.

The party went on for hours. As the room started to empty Nina was seen mingling with everyone, popping for a chat every now and again. Freya had stuck to water all night as she had promised herself, in order not to make a fool of herself at parties anymore. They laughed, danced and socialised with the guests discussing wedding ideas and the all-important hen party.

*

"Hey girls," Nina spoke as she sat down for the first time throughout the party, *Prosecco* in hand. "Have you had a nice time?" she queried.

"It's been great, you have lovely family and friends between you both," Chloe spoke.

"There's some really hot guys here, Nina, can I sit on their table at the wedding?" Louise laughed.

Nina laughed. "Didn't you walk in with a good-looking beefcake?" she questioned.

She glanced at Freya, Nina noticing. "What have I missed?"

"It's nothing. It's not the place. It's your party, we can all catch up another time," Freya spoke.

"No, I want gossip now," she demanded. "Come, on let's go sit in the lounge, nearly everyone's gone, we can catch up now." Nina stood, ushering them from the kitchen seating area.

They walked into a cosy living room, decorated with warm colours, a large brown suede sofa and cuddle swivel chair and the walls caped with photos of Nina and Ben's life together, their childhoods, travelling, holidays and special memories; their life looked like a fairy-tale. Nina grabbed another bottle of *Prosecco* and some blankets from the unit beneath the large TV for them to snuggle into.

As they each removed their heels and sank into the comfy chairs they relaxed. Popping open the bottle, pouring them all a glass, passing them round, Nina sat relieved her hosting was over.

"Come on then, who was the beefcake, Louise?" Nina eagerly waited for her story.

She glanced to Freya who was sipping her *Prosecco*, nibbling on the canapés which were left over.

"That was Chris."

"Chris, as in the personal trainer Chris, the one Freya fancied?" she questioned.

"Yes that's him," Freya sighed.

"So you're dating him now, Louise? And you're not, Freya?" Nina asked, confused.

"Well… Ye, I like him, but now I've seen a different side to him I'm not so sure." She shrugged her shoulders. "He told me it didn't work between you, but failed to mention you to have a restraining order against him."

"What!" Nina excitedly asked. "This is juicy, how come we didn't know?"

Freya put her head down, feeling ashamed, and explained, "Within the past few weeks shit hit the fan, the summer became a blur of drinking and spending time with four different guys. I know it sounds bad." She paused as they gazed upon her. "Like you always say, I got wrapped up in all these men and it bit me in the butt, now I'm trying to get back on top without a man in tow," she went on.

"Explain…"

Freya went on, "As you know I was into Chris, who wouldn't be? He's nice to look at and he seemed so perfect at first. So I don't blame you, Louise, for dating him," looking over at her, smiling. "Although I did question why he was single… it wasn't until I took him as my date to my awards ceremony and he got jealous of Matt which ended with us arguing. He accused Matt of fancying me and punched him!" She paused.

"Oh my god, poor Matt," Chloe added, having liked Matt from before.

"He turned into a right dick within five minutes. I told him to cool off and he left, I ended up falling asleep pissed and woke up in Matt's hotel room," she smirked.

"Ooooooh no, you didn't?" Nina asked.

"No, I slept, he just looked after me and drove me home the next morning. Anyways Chris apologised and admitted he gets jealous over other guys near 'his' women. I didn't like how smothered I felt so I called it off and that was that.

"So I thought… After we had our last catch up round Chloe's I got home to find Matt drunk and asleep on my doorstep."

"You have kept all this to yourself and didn't think to tell us!!!" Louise spoke.

"I know, I know, I'm sorry," Freya apologised. "Anyways, he had been on a date, it didn't end well. The bitch stole his wallet and phone... Some psycho offline," she exhaled. "He knew where I lived as he dropped me off that time and as he had no money or phone and he didn't know where else to go... I let him crash on the sofa and I drove him home the next morning. I did forget he was there though until I walked downstairs in my tiny hot-pant pyjamas," she chuckled.

"You did, didn't you?" Chloe impatiently asked. "After all this time?!"

She grinned. "Well I hadn't planned to, until I was in the shower and he literally joined me!!"

"What the frick!!" Chloe bellowed.

"Nooooo, he didn't!" Louise laughed.

"I know, and I let him! I fancied him for so long, so ye, I slept with him," she admitted. "Anyways I took him home and we exchanged numbers."

"Where does Chris fit into this?" Louise asked with nervousness of how to continue her relationship with him.

"I'm getting there..." She sipped her drink. "That day I then got a text from Jack."

"Now Jack! He's still around?" Nina asked.

"Well I don't think he is now," Freya sighed. "He was back that weekend and it was his mum's birthday party. He asked me to go along... so I did. It was nice to see everyone from school, his friends and family, I enjoyed myself.

"Anyway he drove to mine and picked me up and as I was getting in the car, Chris appeared shouting nasty stuff at me about how he saw Matt leave and then saw Jack pick me up, so yes, I get it, it looked bad on my behalf and Jack heard the lot," she admitted, embarrassed.

"He saw Matt?" Chloe questioned.

"It turns out he's been stalking me for a bit and was near my house that morning and then again that afternoon.

"I told him to leave and back off and he was getting aggressive. Jack was watching from the car then got out and stepped in and Jack ended up punching him."

"He punched that massive guy!" Nina exclaimed.

"I know, it wasn't just a punch though, Chris retaliated and they ended up having a proper street fight which then attracting all the neighbours and the police."

"Oh Freya," Louise spoke.

"They were both arrested. Jack's been giving a warning and a fine from the army, which I feel awful about, and Chris was given a restraining order to stay away from me," she finished.

"Wow, I'm sorry we haven't been there for you, you should have just texted us," Chloe told her.

"Nah, I'm fine, don't worry about it," Freya said.

"Where does that leave you and Jack?" Nina questioned.

"Well we had a great time at the party and I stayed over that night." Looking upon their facial expressions she didn't need to tell them they were intimate.

"In the morning I told him we couldn't have what he wanted due to the distance."

Nina went to speak. "I know, Nina, you don't need to say it. I'm stupid and I really do sound like a slut. We ended up arguing, he point-blank told me I was messing around with all these men, stringing him along and wasted my summer. He reminded me I hadn't been on any interviews or got a job in place like I had planned, and he's right. He told me to leave, so I did and cried all the way home." Louise hugged her as she saw Freya's mood change.

"It's fine, I think I needed it. I have applied for jobs all week and have a week of interviews lined up, I'm excited. I haven't heard from Jack and I doubt he wants me to contact him which makes me sad but now I am eager to get my career started and start fresh." She smiled.

"That's fabulous news, Freya," Nina excitedly added.

"What jobs are they?" Louise questioned.

"There's a few sports management roles, a sports therapist, stuff like that using the skills which I learnt within my course. Although Matt emailed me saying he got me an interview at the university alongside the sports departments which I can do my teaching course alongside." She shrugged.

"That sounds perfect," Chloe spoke.

"It does, I am going to go, but I do feel like I may have only earned it by sleeping with him. Then there is the question, do I really want to work with someone I have slept with?" she asked for insight.

"It'll be fine, I think you should go for it. It's the perfect job, it would suit you down to a tee, just remember to be professional, which won't be hard as you have been for the past three years already," Nina insisted.

"Ye, I suppose, although it may be harder now he is undiscovered and you were right about the kissing, Chloe," she laughed. "Thank you, girls, I feel so much better now I have finally vented."

"Can I just add something?" Nina probed.

"Go on." They all looked towards her.

"I think you should message Jack and end on better terms. I've always hoped you two would end up together," she admitted.

"I know you have, maybe I will write to him," Freya suggested, smiling as she sipped on her one and only glass of *Prosecco*.

They chatted into the next morning where they ended up sleeping in Nina's spare bedroom which they hadn't done in years.

CHAPTER 12

He's Back

Spending the next few days drinking plenty and eating healthy, she tapered her running schedule ready for her marathon next Saturday, having planned a few short runs for the beginning of the week then a few days off in order to reduce the chances of burning out. She had been round friends and family plus a collection pot had been sent round in the bar, all in order to get some sponsors for her chosen charity, being Help for Heroes for obvious reasons. She stood staring at the amount she had raised once it was all counted up. She was shocked by how much support she had and was now more eager than ever to complete the miles. After all this was the first and most likely only marathon she was going to do. Having only stated she was going to raise £1,000, she was proud to be able to donate more. Once she had finished sorting out she wrote a cheque to post along with a letter.

Hi Jack

I don't know where to start, but I hope you are ok.

I'm sorry about the way things ended between us after such a nice time we had together, I am completely to blame and I feel awful about it. I am not surprised you have not contacted me, I wouldn't want to talk to me either.

You of all people know me better than anyone, probably even more than I do myself. After you opened my eyes to my shameful behaviour I completely agree with you. I have been a complete fool this summer and I think I relaxed a little too much and forgot about the plan I had before. Which I know isn't an excuse.

Anyway I feel better about myself now that I can tell you I have interviews all this week! They're mainly sports jobs plus one at my university where I can also do my teacher training. It sounded interesting so I'm going along for the interview, fingers crossed I have a job offer once summer is over.

I also have my marathon next Saturday too. I know you can't come to cheer me on but please think of me as in this heat I can see it being a struggle plus the lack of training, I only managed to get to 20 miles so the last 6 I will have to use my pure will power to achieve. I have managed to raise £1700 how good is that?! I have donated it to help for heroes like I spoke about in the past. You will also find a cheque enclosed for £700 for your fine as it was my fault and you don't deserve to be punished. After all you were being my hero at the time. I'm hoping to make amends so please don't be too proud to take it.

Anyway I have to go, I hope you're ok

Love Freya

Xoxox

She addressed the letter, put her shoes on and walked to the post box feeling like she had another thing ticked off her list. As the music played through her headphones the lyrics and old songs took her back to past memories with Jack which made her hope he would respond soon. After all, she had never seemed to be able to get over him and not knowing if they were still friends pulled on her heart strings.

The sun was shining down on her bare tanned skin making her feel warm. Her tan made her look like she had been away abroad, which made her wish she had been able to relax with a cocktail by the beach watching the waves. The street seemed quiet considering it was nearing the end of the summer; then again it was only 9am. Freya was on a mission today; she had a hair appointment for the first time in forever, it felt, and was also booked in for her nails prior to her first interview at the university tomorrow.

As she walked to her usual hairdresser's she was the only one in there. Although it was usually closed on a Tuesday she felt privileged they opened for her. Following her new outlook on life as a working woman she recently found herself searching for new hairstyles and was considering a change to discard her days of university and bad choices.

"Morning Freya," Lucy spoke as the bell rang with the door opening, smiling as usual.

"Hey, how are you?" she replied.

"I'm alright, thank you, how about you? I can't believe it's been so long, where have you been?"

"I know, it's been a while, my hair is definitely due a treatment. I can't wait for a pamper."

As she put on her gown, she took her mug of tea and sat down, staring herself in the mirror. Noticing her hair having become ridiculously longer than usual, she definitely had let it go.

"What are we doing? The usual wash and trim?" Lucy queried as she played with her hair.

"Well actually I was thinking about a change," she spoke with a grin.

"Oh, intriguing, something different for a change? That's a surprise," Lucy questioned.

"I know, I know, I feel like I need a new look for the new me. I've finished university and I am now going in full force to become an independent working woman once I get a job offer." She smiled towards Lucy in the mirror.

"Sounds good, what are you thinking?"

Freya took her phone out and showed her some photos she had recently screenshot from the internet.

"This will look great on you. I can't wait, and I love a new style," Lucy excitedly said as she grabbed the hair dye pots.

She opened her heart to Lucy like any normal girl would do with their hairdresser; she felt surer of her plans for the near future. Lucy giving an opinion as an outsider sure did help. As she drank plenty of cups of tea and pints of water whilst snacking on fruit and nuts peace flowed through her body. She caught up on the latest celebrity gossip, reading magazine after magazine for nearly three hours which consisted of hair treatments, a head massage, a colour and cut. Now eager to see her new hair she nervously bit the inside of her lip as Lucy started to blow dry, revealing her new colour. Having always been brunette she was feeling brave having added some colour onto her hair and having not told anyone they would surely be in for surprise.

"I think it suits you, you look more stunning than ever and it really complements your tan," Lucy said as she showed Freya the back in her handheld mirror.

Freya stared, gazing at her new look, stunned with how much she liked it. She beamed.

"I'm really pleased with it, thank you so much. Who knew a splash of blonde balayage would make such a drastic change?" She grinned as she looked back and forth into the mirror. "I love it!" she squealed.

"You're welcome, I've enjoyed doing it."

As she paid and bid farewell to Lucy she enjoyed her short walk through the town to the nail salon, checking her new hair in the shop windows as she passed them. She couldn't help but smile back at herself now her newly dyed hair made her look freshly sun-kissed and well looked after. Having spent the next two hours in the nail salon having girly chats with other clients and her nail technician, Freya felt happy with her end result of a freshly painted French manicure to match her newly lightened hair. Feeling completely relaxed and pampered she made her way home ready for her interview in the morning, looking as good as ever in case she bumped into Matt.

*

Beep, beep, beep. A sound she hadn't heard for nearly six weeks woke her with a startle. Having spent the night prepping for her interview she seemed to have fallen into a deep sleep for the first time in a while. A 7am start for a 9am interview was surely enough to get her back into a normal routine for when her career started. She climbed out of bed feeling relaxed although quite nervous; butterflies swirled her stomach made her feel slightly nauseous.

Whilst the kettle boiled she skimmed the news, flicked through her phone and made some toast. As her hair was freshly washed yesterday all she needed was to run some straighteners through it, do her make-up and get dressed. Hanging on the door was a long, high-waisted grey pencil skirt with a white shirt which had been freshly ironed last night.

Having never interviewed before and being completely used to the sports attire, she was pleased to find some old shirts she used to wear for work at the bar which would do, although her blouse hung slightly big due to her recent weight loss. She dug through her drawers and took out a large wide belt, tucked her shirt into her skirt, wrapping her belt around her slim waist which complemented her outfit choice which she finished with some black kitten heels. It seems she had picked up a thing or two from Chloe being the fashion expert.

Freya stood before her full-length mirror feeling ready to go. Still smiling at her new look, her nails glistened, her hair was shining and her body looked great in her opinion. She was hoping Matt was going to like her new look if she bumped into him. Her eyeliner was blunt around her eyes and her lashes long; the blackness made her eyes stand out above her freckled cheeks and red lips.

*

8:15am soon rolled round. She grabbed her bag

filled with all her required information including her updated CV, qualifications and forms of identification. She locked the door and drove to her recent university campus. Pulling into the car park, she reminisced about her fond memories as a student. Having missed the atmosphere she was feeling excited to go back in through the doors as a graduate never having to take a dreaded exam again, although her heartbeat raised within her chest, her palms felt sweaty and butterflies swirled her stomach at the thought of the interview. As her heels tapped against the tiles she made her way to reception. Eyeing up the clock, 8:50am, she glanced around the room to find it was quiet. Due to it being the holidays no students were in sight, instead lecturers were dotted around preparing for their teacher-training days and planning prior to the new term starting.

"Hi," she nervously spoke to the receptionist with a pause as she looked up. "I'm here for an interview at 9am, I'm Freya Bell."

The receptionist rose from behind the desk and made her way to Freya.

"Morning Freya, we have been expecting you. I believe your interviewing with Mr Jones, please follow me." She smiled as she walked her through the campus.

Her heart sank as she heard his name. Feeling a blush upon her cheeks she tried to breathe slowly to calm herself down.

Holy shit, she thought as she made her way up the stairs, feeling complete déjà vu.

"Here we are, just take a seat here." She directed

her to the seats outside the sports office. "I'll let him know you have arrived."

Having spent the last three years at the campus, it seemed Ellen the receptionist didn't recognise her at all considering they had had plenty of conversations in the early mornings. *Maybe it's my hair and non-sports attire, or she's being professional,* she thought as she took a cup of ice-cold water from the dispenser nearby.

"Morning Mr Jones, I have Freya Bell outside for your first interview of the day," she heard her say around the door.

First? Oh no! The thought of being against others hadn't even crossed her mind. She felt nauseous, feeling like the interview was a complete waste of time as she felt unqualified for a lecturing role in the first place, especially as she disliked speaking in front of people.

As she stood wanting to leave Matt appeared from the office fiddling with his shirt buttons, seeming like he had only just got dressed.

"Miss Bell," he spoke with a friendly gesture and smile, shaking her hand as others looked on.

As she took his hand she caught on he was acting as professional as he could around his colleagues. The tension between them sparked feelings within her loins which took her back to the last time she saw him. *He was butt naked in my shower,* she thought as she bit her lip.

"Morning Mr Jones, please call me Freya." She blushed.

"OK Freya. Would you like to come into my

office?" he directed as he opened the door, holding it open for her.

As she made her way into the room she was relieved to see no one else was interviewing alongside him. Having never been in his office she observed the way he had decorated it with photos of his sports achievements and qualifications hung on the walls. His desk full of paperwork beside an empty cup. He pulled out the chair beneath her where she sat opposite him, she now felt like a school girl all over again. The large brown desk separating them made her body tingle; she wanted him more than ever, now she couldn't have him. He smelt freshly showered and looked recently groomed. She fancied him so much right now and having seen what was under his clothes made it harder to push aside her horniness. Trying to stay professional she shook away her naughty thoughts, now knowing working with Matt if successful would be impossible.

"Thanks for coming, Freya." He paused as he shuffled with his paperwork, looking as nervous as she felt, which was unlike him.

The room fell silent for what seemed like forever, her heels tapped on the chair leg as they shook as she sat feeling uncomfortable, unsure of what so say to break the awkwardness.

"Thank you for getting me an interview," she spoke to break the silence. "Here are my certificates, form of identification and current CV." She slid them across the table towards Matt. He reached out for them, their fingers touching, making her eyes gaze into his. She was feeling hot for him; from the look in his eyes he wanted her too.

For the first time she could see in his face he was struggling to hide his feelings like he had for the last three years. His breathing was raised, his body language was distant, his eyes were burning into her. He was silent, and unable to focus. He seemed lost within his thoughts. She wished she knew what he was thinking. "Err, thank you, Freya. Sorry, can you give me a minute?" he tensely spoke as he stood from his chair and quickly walked out of the room.

Freya let out a heavy breath, slumping down into her chair for a second, her mind screaming at her to get a grip although that seemed quite impossible for her unless Matt did too. Her nails quickly tapped on the desk as her knees trembled, unsure of what to do.

The door opened behind her; she sat straight back up, turning towards Matt, who quickly made his way back behind the desk between them.

"Right, so the position is a sports lecturer. It's a full-time job during term times with a few training days here and there. Here is the job description, training schedule and pay grade details. Take a look through that," he spoke, passing her paper, now not looking up at her. He continued to speak at a much faster rate than normal, in a rush for the interview to be over. Feeling confused she sat nodding her head as she watched his curious behaviour. She also could not wait to leave.

"For the first year you will work alongside another lecturer whilst you complete your teacher training. I'm unsure who the lecturer will be at this time but I'll find out for you. The course is fully funded and your placement would also be here so it's easily done, let's say it's basically a guaranteed job whilst qualifying rather than the usual university course with placement after which you then need to find a job. We're basically making a teacher out of you on the job. How does it all sound?" He paused, taking a sip of his now full cup of coffee.

"It all sounds great, I never really thought about lecturing if I'm honest but it does sound like it ticks all the right boxes for a long career within the sports sector," she spoke towards him. He was not making eye contact.

"I know you have more interviews later and I have a few lined up this week also, do you know when the decision is being made?" she asked, waiting in an awkward silence.

Lifting his head, finally looking her in the eyes, he smiled.

"Freya, the job is yours if you want it," he responded with a smile. Unsure of what to say, Freya felt like she hadn't earnt the job or even participated in an actual interview. Confused, she felt the need to ask what was going on. Dropping the professionalism, she responded.

"Matt, can I call you Matt?" she queried.

He nodded. "Yes Freya, I'm not your teacher anymore, remember?"

"Ye, about that, I don't want to be given a job based on what is happening or what has happened between us, shall I say. I want to feel like I've earned it. Otherwise I've done my course for no reason, I don't want it handed to me," she bluntly explained.

Matt, looking stunned, rose from his chair, making

his way around the desk as Freya stayed within her chair following him with her eyes.

"No, Freya, it's not based on that at all," he expressed. "I do not want you to think that is the reason I invited you for this interview, as it wasn't me who first initiated it anyway." He paused. He sat upon the desk beside Freya, looking down at her as he spoke. "If it makes you feel better I can arrange another member of staff to interview you and all the candidates, that way my feelings for you are obsolete in the choice," he calmly spoke towards her. "Would that make you feel happier?" he asked with his arms crossed, seeming a lot more relaxed than he did earlier.

"Yes, yes it really would," she smiled.

"Good, come back at the end of the day around 2pm then, once everyone else has been interviewed," he requested, looking at his watch.

"Thank you, Matt, I really appreciate it."

Freya stood from her chair, pulling down her skirt as she rose, picked up her paperwork and made for the door, feeling Matt watch her every move.

"Right, I'm glad that's sorted." He walked over to the door to walk her out, and as he went for the handle instead of opening it he locked it. Before she knew it Matt had grabbed her by the waist, turning her body towards his with his hand in her hair, planting a kiss hard onto her lips, smudging every bit of lipstick. He kissed her like he meant it. Startled, Freya stood taken aback, allowing him until her body allowed her to respond. Placing her hands behind his neck, their tongues entwined. Allowing her to take a breath Matt retreated, stepping back, adjusting his hard cock within his tight suit trousers.

"Sorry, I couldn't help myself, you look amazing. I love your new hair and your tits look so hot in that shirt," he smirked.

His honesty and use of words made her horny; she felt her usual instincts kicking in, making her want to pounce on him whilst she was in the moment, unsure if he would allow it his office.

She was the one who was now silent.

Staring at each other, they both knew what they wanted. Unable to wait for Matt to make the move, she moved back in for more. Kissing him hard, she moved his body to the table with all her force as he moved willingly with her. Unbuckling his belt and undoing his button she felt his sigh of relief as his erection fell free. Knowing they were in distance of being heard and short for time she had never felt so turned on in her life. Feeling naughty, her clit pulsed. Eager to get her hands on his bulge, she made her way quickly down his boxers, stimulating his cock as he moaned with enjoyment. Trying not to ruin her perfect rhythm Matt lifted up her skirt allowing her white lacy thong to be on show, her pert buttocks looking good enough for him to nibble on. Lowering her underwear, she stepped out of them. As he sat on the edge of the table his length stood hard, ready for her. She straddled him, his hard cock sliding into her entrance with ease. Gasping at the feeling shooting through her body, she was shocked she climaxed so suddenly. Trying to moan quietly, he allowed her body to release her tension before picking her up with her legs wrapped around his body, placing her on her back on the edge of the desk. He thrusted hard into her sex with her groaning at each pulse. Her body losing control numerous times made his cock harder, making him work faster to see the pleasure in her face. Biting down on her lip trying to control her sounds, she felt completely in awe of the moment. Aggravated she couldn't see his abs or touch his skin due to his skirt being on, she pulled on his clothes, pulling him closer, sliding her hands up his shirt, gliding her nails down his back, firmly grasping his ass as he thrusted hard into her.

He quickened, ready to ejaculate, letting out a deep breath, slowing his movements as he looked down at her. Unable to move she let her legs drop over the table with her heels still tightly secure on her feet. Looking down at herself, her outfit now completely screwed up, her hair felt a mess and her lips smudged. As Matt sorted himself out he placed a hand out towards her pulling her up. After catching her breath she sat upright. Grabbing her bag she took her compact mirror and made herself look presentable in order to leave the room. Standing up, adjusting her clothes, she could feel his juices within her pussy which ached with delight. Feeling completely satisfied, her smile now beamed.

"I feel much better now I've got that off my mind," Matt said.

"Something was on your mind?" she questioned sarcastically. "I couldn't tell," she laughed.

"Ha, sorry," he smiled.

"That was amazing. I've had that image in my head for the last three years," she responded.

"Me too," he grinned.

He tidied his desk, making sure it looked as it had done, smoothed out her hair, kissed her on the cheek and unlocked the door.

"I want to see you more often," he confessed.

She looked up at him before stepping out of the room; her face beamed. "You can," she whispered.

As they exited the room she felt relieved no one was outside who would have heard their sexy time.

"See you later, Freya," Matt spoke as he made his way towards the staff room, giving her a sly wink. She made her way down the stairs, her inner thighs still tingling. She had just about calmed down once she made it back to her car. Looking at her watch it was only 10:15am, another four hours until she had to come back for a real interview. She sat in her car deciding what to do until 2pm as she would rather not go home again. As she flicked through her CDs; she played some 90s classics and made her way out of the car park, singing along with the windows down without a care in the world as to who could hear her. She decided to go to the shopping centre nearby for some new clothes.

She parked up her car and collected her parking ticket. She walked towards the shops; as she mooched around going from shop to shop she had bought several new items including shoes, new clothes and new underwear. She rarely treated herself but today she was in a great mood. As she finished paying for some new matte lipstick she felt her stomach rumble, checking the time, and made her way to a nearby café for some lunch. Having always preferred the independent businesses compared to the popular chains she often chose the café Nineties due to its warm feeling, menu choice and friendly owners. She walked in and went straight to her favourite seat in the corner next to the window.

"Afternoon Freya, how lovely to see you," Joe spoke as she stood and gave him a kiss on the cheek.

"Hi Joe, I'm good thank you, how about you? How is Hannah holding up in this heat? Is the baby here yet?" she responded.

"No baby yet, any day I hope, she is alright resting at home. If it was her choice she would be here until she popped," he laughed.

"Bless her. Well I hope the baby comes soon, send her my love."

"I will do, would you like your usual?" he queried.

"Yes please," she smiled.

"Got it, I'll catch up later," he spoke as he walked away.

"Thanks Joe."

Freya sat reading the magazines whilst chatting to the customers she knew and watching the people rushing by outside doing their everyday routines. Sipping her tea and finishing her salad she spotted a handsome fella walking towards the café. She found herself grinning as he walked in the door. As he went to the counter he observed the seating and looked upon her, smiling. She gave him a slight wave as he took his drink, pointed to her table and made his way over.

"I get the pleasure of seeing you twice in one day?" Matt spoke.

"Hi," she smiled. "Ye, I didn't go home, I've been shopping and grabbed some lunch before heading back over," she explained.

"Treating yourself I see," he spoke, observing her Miss Selfridge, TK Maxx and Topshop bags.

"Sure have."

"I have two blueberry muffins here for you, sir," Joe spoke as he stood at her table.

"Just here, thank you," as he pulled out the chair opposite her.

"Enjoy," Joe spoke as he placed them down, smiling at Freya.

"Thank you, Joe." She smirked.

"So you come in here often?" Matt asked.

"Can you tell? I love it in here, it's my favourite place to come for some me time whilst enjoying the nice food, plus I get to watch everyone outside," she went on.

"I agree, I come here often too," he spoke, taking a bite out of his muffin. "Soo, about earlier," Matt went onto explain.

"No need to apologise, I know it's awkward," she butted in.

"I'm going to be straight with you. I really like you, I think you're super sexy and I'm interested in getting to know you. I know you have some boy dramas going on and I don't want to be a rebound or get into something messy." He paused. "Are you interested in me?" He straightforwardly asked. "Obviously I know you fancy me, you told me that unconsciously and we have now had sex twice unplanned and unprotected which is not something I do often. There is just something about you which makes me unable to control myself, but if you don't want it to be more than just sex I think we need to be on the same page," he honestly spoke.

She finished her muffin as she listened, leaving her unsure of how to respond. After all, at the weekend she had decided she wanted to focus on a career and take a break from men and now Matts making it clear he wants some sort of relationship.

"What do you mean unconsciously?" was all she managed to process.

"Ha, you made a comment on the way back to my hotel room when you were passed out at the awards ceremony." He grinned, awaiting the reply he wanted.

"Oh how embarrassing," placing her hand over her face, hiding her embarrassment. "Honestly, I wasn't expecting this to happen. I thought you were going to be my university crush which I never got to have and never see you again once I left. Yes, I have the major hots for you, I have done for three years and now I've had a taste of you I want more." She paused.

"I don't just sleep around with guys if that's what you think. This summer has been the worst my love life has been and what's happened has not been intentional, I promise you that. We haven't had sex unprotected. I'm on the coil, if that was your polite way of asking me. I would never do that and I am clean too if you needed to know," she sharply spoke. "If we're being honest then you best get another drink and I can explain myself, as there is no way I'm

195

leaving with you thinking all I want from you is sex because it's not. Although I do only have an hour," she spoke, looking at the time.

As Freya took the time to explain about Chris, Jack and even Bradley she felt better to finally have a moment of clarity, even more so with a guy she was genuinely interested in. Having told him her concerns about working together should she be successful, he reassured her it wouldn't be awkward if they were on the same page.

He went on to explain he had only been with one girl in the past who he was engaged to but it didn't work out and hadn't found anyone due to his bad decision of trying online dating. He was open about his concern for her feelings for Jack, although she assured him there wasn't anything to worry about due to him not talking to her anymore.

"So, dinner tonight? 6:30pm, I'll pick you up," Matt asked.

"Perfect. Right, I best go," Freya responded. They stood to leave. Matt paid, refusing to let her pay, and they walked out together. "Bye Joe." She waved as she left.

"See you, good luck in your marathon at the weekend!" he shouted across the room.

"Thank you," she smiled.

They chatted as they walked toward the car park; he gave her tips about her interview although it still sounded like she had the job already by the way he was speaking.

As he walked her to her car he handed her

shopping bags to her. "Good luck." He kissed her on the cheek.

"Thank you," she smiled as she climbed into the driver's seat.

"See you later," she heard as she shut the door, giving him a wave as she drove off.

CHAPTER 13

First Date

Following her interview she was feeling much better about her effort to earn the job as a sports lecturer. After discussing the role in much more depth with the sports head Mr Smith, she now wanted the job more than ever as it was perfect for her, teaching the subject she loved, with the perfect hours, with the opportunity to progress into a long-term career and working alongside people she knew. She already felt at home within the campus. She was advised she would hear within the week if she had been successful which made her anxious every time she opened her emails.

Unsure if Matt was more laid back about the interview approach or was being extra nice to her, she had to partake in a few assessments which without warning she felt she did the best she could. As she found she was one of three being interviewed for the position she didn't really feel 100 percent reassured she would be successful so she planned to prepare for her next two interviews tomorrow.

Following a ten-mile run she showered and dolled

herself up ready for her date with Matt, who after today she was officially 'dating' which still sounded unbelievable to her as he seemed so perfect for her. She wore her new white lace thong with a matching bra which she was sure to be revealing later underneath a new outfit and her new shoes. She flaunted her bust in a low-cut body suit which showed every curve of her upper body, accompanied with high-waisted jeans which made her look as trim as she ever had been before. Every outline was on show. As she looked in her mirror upon herself she liked what she saw, hoping Matt would too. As she finished her make-up she curled her hair. Her newly streaked blonde hair bounced as she made her way downstairs. Matt was due within the next 15 minutes; she pottered around tidying her kitchen and she sipped some wine as she opened her laptop and reloaded her emails. Matt knocked on the door as she opened an email subject marked 'Interview' which churned her stomach.

"It's open!" she shouted as she skim read the email.

Dear Freya

I am writing to confirm an offer as a Training Sports Lecturer within the Sports department at our university campus.

The hours will be 32 hours per week for 40 weeks of the year plus teacher training days.

This position is offered subject to satisfactory reference and pre-employment checks and completion of the six-month probation period during which time your performance will be reviewed. As a full member of staff you will therefore be entitled to all staff benefits.

Your starting date will be 29th August should you accept this offer.

Please confirm your acceptance of the position as soon as possible so we can continue with the clearance checks.

We are looking forward to working with you and hope you will soon feel part of the team. If you have any questions, please contact me.

Mr L Smith

Head of Sports Department

She shut her laptop as Matt made his way into the kitchen. "Hey, beautiful." He kissed her cheek, handing her a single red rose.

"Hey," she beamed.

"You look gorgeous," he complimented.

Turning towards him, Freya felt like she was in a bubble; she felt happy and excited about her future with a job offer on the table and now dating 'the hot teacher' she never thought she would.

She couldn't stop smiling, keeping her silent. "You alright?" he queried her silence.

"I'm perfect," she responded, planting a kiss upon his lips. He responded without thought, her hands on his face, feeling his slightly prickly jawline, making her way around the back of his neck, holding him close to her. His hands moving up and down her body, feeling every inch with one hand within her curls. Their tongues interlacing with each other, lifting her from the floor, wrapping her legs around him as he placed her on the kitchen unit. Her pussy numb from wanting him badly as she felt his erection against her from within his jeans. Her hands slid up his shirt, feeling his warm body, her kisses upon his neck as he responded. He paused, looking at her, amused.

"We have to go, table's at 7:00," he smirked.

"You're joking?" she asked, laughing.

"Come on." He took her off the side and kissed her forehead. "Anyway I don't have sex on the first date," he joked.

"Oh really... We will see about that," she informed.

He grabbed her hand, making their way to the door to leave. The evening seemed cooler tonight; she grabbed a light jacket and locked the door. "Let's walk?" he suggested. "OK?"

She nodded.

They walked the ten minutes to the restaurant hand in hand. Making conversation with him came so easily; it felt effortlessness which she liked. Having also started on an honest open page helped make her feel at ease in his company. Arriving into the food court, it seemed Wednesday was a busy evening as couples and families were seen within the streets making their way to or from dinner. Walking towards the Italian restaurant Freya heard a familiar voice hollering towards her.

"Freya?"

"Louise..."

She let go of Matt's hand, giving Louise a hug. "Hey, you alright? What you doing out on a week day?" she giggled.

"Louise, this is Matt," she introduced as they shook hands. "We're on a date," she smiled.

"Ooh, finally I get to meet the famous hot teacher." She openly laughed as she puffed on a cigarette, exhaling the smoke.

He smirked. "Well I didn't realise I was famous," glancing at Freya as she blushed, shrugging her shoulders, gazing back at him.

"What? I told you I had a huge crush on you, of course I told my girlfriends! Are you here for dinner too?" Freya probed.

As she dabbed her cigarette in the ashtray she looked at Freya, concerned.

"Ye, I am, but I'm with Chris." She paused. "He's inside." She grinned, biting her teeth together, expecting to upset Freya.

She glanced through the window, as did Matt. Luckily he was out of sight. He grabbed her hand. "It's alright Freya, we can eat somewhere else, there are plenty to choose from," he reassured her.

"If that's OK? We could have Mexican? Do you like Mexican?" she questioned.

"One of my favourites," he agreed.

"Sorry Freya," Louise butted in as she observed Freya and Matt's blossoming relationship.

"It's fine, Louise, don't apologise. So you're actually dating?" she queried.

"Ye, we have been, it's going well. I do really like him," she admitted, looking into the restaurant.

Freya could see Chris making his way towards the door.

"OK, well I'll let you go." She kissed Louise on the cheek, hugging her goodbye "I hope he's being nicer to you than he was to me," she whispered over her shoulder.

"Don't worry, I have got that sorted," she responded.

"Love you, enjoy your night," Freya spoke as she grabbed Matt's hand and headed in the opposite direction before Chris saw them. She definitely wasn't in the mood for him to pop her bubble today.

"Babe, what's the hold-up?" She heard Chris' manly voice, not looking back at them.

"Sorry Matt, I hope you weren't fancying Italian too much," she apologetically spoke.

"Don't worry about it, I'll eat anything." He smiled at her as held the door to the Mexican restaurant open.

Thoroughly enjoying her first proper date with Matt, they chatted about their lives, getting to know one another properly, making each other laugh whilst they found out what they had in common and became friends for the first time in three years.

"Shall we head off?" Matt asked as he took the last sip of his drink.

"Ye, I'll just nip to the toilet," she responded.

"I'll pay and meet you outside."

"OK, thank you."

Buzz, buzz, buzz. Freya's phone vibrated within her

bag. Matt took her phone out to see who was calling.

The screen lit up reading 'JACK'. As Freya walked towards the door Matt placed her phone back in her bag, discarding the call. "All sorted?" he asked, failing to mention the call as he passed her bag back to her. "Ye, all good," she smiled, retrieving her bag.

He took her hand as they walked back to her house.

As she unlocked the door Freya knew she wanted to have Matt upstairs in her bed, but his mood seemed to have changed along the way back which she had become aware of, unsure what she had done wrong.

"Do you fancy some more dessert?" she cheekily grinned as they walked into the hallway.

"I told you earlier, I don't on the first date," he shyly responded.

Taken aback, she did not know what to do or say. Being turned down was not something she was used to.

"What's wrong? Something changed on the way back?" she openly queried as she sat on the stairs removing her shoes.

"I've had a great day, I am having a great time with you. Something is just playing on my mind but I don't want to ruin our date by sounding like a jerk," he explained.

"I really don't think you could be a jerk if you're just honest with me like we were this morning," she probed.

He leaned with his back against the front door, sighing heavily.

"OK, I've acted like a dick. Your phone rang when you were in the bathroom and I didn't mention anything as it made me feel a little awkward. I don't want you to think I'm jealous like Chris but I want to have you to myself, although it doesn't feel like I can," he spoke, ashamed as she scanned her phone, finding a missed call and voicemail from Jack. She breathed out after realising she was holding her breath as she listened. Her stomach flipped just at the sight of his name. Freya could see in Matt's behaviour he was being genuine, he seemed like he was really interested in her and had been completely sincere all day. She knew her and Jack would never happen and she needed to abandon any idea of it happening as they'd had their chance to be together. She sat with Matt opposite her, scanned her phone and deleted the unheard voicemail and placed it down.

She stood up, walking towards him.

She kissed his lips; he did not react. His body stood straight against the door, stiff whilst looking down at her. She gazed into his eyes. "Matt, I told you this morning there is nothing to worry about. Me and Jack are in the past. I'm pretty sure he was only calling to wish me luck for the marathon next week. Right now I honestly only have interest in one person and he is standing right in front of me. I want to talk to him all the time, look at him, touch him and taste him." She said, flirting as she went to kiss his neck. He smiled, placing his hands on her waist as he enjoyed her begging. "I also bought some nice new underwear just for you today if you would like to see?" she pleaded.

"Oh really?" he smirked as she nibbled his neck.

He took his hand underneath her jaw, moving her head for a kiss. "I'll break my rule on no sex on the first date on one condition," he queried.

"What condition would that be?" she asked, intrigued, as she groped his hard cock over his jeans.

He paused, stopped her hand, picked her up and carried her up the stairs.

"I don't want to fuck you, I want to make love to you," he demanded.

He pushed open the bedroom door, placing her on the bed. "Stay here," he requested.

"Where you going?" she worriedly quizzed as she sat up.

"I will be back in a minute," he reassured her as he walked out of the door with a grin on his face.

Her mind ran with curiosity. *Where has he gone? What does he mean make love to me?* Come to think of it, had she even ever made love? Every sexual activity she encountered was usually spontaneous and naughty. Hard fucking with little intimacy, usually not taking place in a bed. Has she been missing out, she wondered? Her palms suddenly felt sweaty. *What if I don't know how to make love? I can't say I have made love with Jack, we were only young and it was more learning what sex was then,* although she felt she loved him. Her mind raced with nerves. She lay on her back with her head in her hands as she tried to stay calm, listening to Matt's footsteps making his way back upstairs. She ran her fingers through her hair and sat back up, smiling at him as he returned.

He returned with candles which he must have

found within her kitchen and a bottle of wine and two glasses. She watched as he drew the curtains to block out the last remaining sunlight; he placed candles upon her unit, lighting them with the igniter from her dresser.

Popping the cork off a bottle of red wine he poured two glasses; he flicked 'play' on his phone which connected to her Bluetooth speakers. As love songs played through the speakers Freya felt nervous, like she was losing her virginity all over again. He placed his hand towards her for her to take. She took it, gripping onto him tightly as he raised her from the bed, pulling her towards him as he handed her a glass of wine. She took a large swig to help ease the anxieties. His eyes locked into hers, looking full of surprises.

"I get the impression you have not had a guy make love to you before?" he timidly asked.

"At this precise moment, I'm unsure," she responded, quickly downing her wine, taking a deep breath out to remove the flavour. Red wine was a drink she never really enjoyed but it helped take the edge off.

He took the glass off her placing it down. His hand reached around her waist as he took the other, linking their fingers. He persuaded her body to sway to the music; within seconds they were dancing to the music as her eyes gazed back into his, as nothing was heard but the soft tune. Their bodies close, still fully clothed, yet her body felt like it was melting against his, she was completely in the moment, feeling utterly adored. He looked down to her until their lips touched; his tongue wrapped around hers and his hand beneath her long thick hair pulling her closer.

Pushing up against her, he guided her to the bed. The room was now dark, lit by just candlelight with the scent of candles filling the air. As she lay beneath him, his hands firmly holding her body as he devoured her mouth, he found she was as hungry for him as he was for her. She felt her pussy fill with essence as she could smell the scent of his testosterone arising from his skin.

Taking a breath, he stared at her as his eyes adjusted to light. She smiled beneath him.

"Can I see your new undies?" he asked as his fingers unbuttoned her jeans.

She nodded, falling silent, kissing him on his warm lips as she rose from the bed. He sat watching her every move as she stood in front of him, finding her confidence, allowing him to watch her slowly lower her jeans. Her playsuit tight against her skin showed the curves of her ass on full show. He licked his lips as she didn't take her eyes off of him. As her hands found her crotch her hair fell around her face; unbuttoning her poppers she lifted her top, revealing her white lacy bra, her breasts looking full. Finding his feet, he grabbed her body. His hands touching her, squeezing her as he admired her. "You're amazing, Freya," he spoke.

Her hands untucked his shirt, pulling it above his head as he worked with her. He dropped his jeans, allowing his hard cock to be free. Her hands groped his dick as his lips kissed her tanned skin. Lowering his boxers, she lowered to her knees, taking his length into her mouth. He gasped, she tasted him, making her pussy fill with sexual fluid. She was more than ready for him, having never felt sexual tension like it.

As his fingers fell deep within her hair he groaned; she sucked him hard, feeling every vein and ripple of his smooth shaved cock.

"Please don't stop doing that," he moaned as she enjoyed herself.

His voice trembled as his body quivered. Slowly stopping, she let go, licked her lips. His body relaxed from his tense stance. Sipping some wine, she wanted him to take charge, she wanted him to make love to her like no one had before. She took a sip, holding it within her mouth. As she locked lips she passed it to Matt who willingly swallowed, his eyes glistening as the candles flickered around them.

"Take me now," she whispered.

Lifting her body with his strong arms, she giggled as she wrapped her legs around him. He carried her back to the bed, placing her down, climbing above her. He kissed her tummy, removing her thong with his teeth, tossing it aside. His kiss made their way up from her toes, up the inside of legs, onto her wet, pulsing clit. She groaned with a pulse of pleasure waiting for the teasing to stop. Making his way up her body he caressed her breasts with his mouth as his fingers unclipped the bra. Her breasts falling free, kissing them, taking her erect nipple into his mouth, nibbling it as she trembled. Spreading her legs, his cock entered her welcoming pussy; he found her warm and moist. She melted against him as she felt the fullness of him entering him. As he thrusted their bodies fell close, she felt part of him, enjoying him, she forgot herself. He was grinding hard into her as the music played around them, their rhythm becoming out of sync as they lost their train of thoughts within each other; all coordination had been lost. Their love-making became harder, he was ready to explode, she wanted it deep within her loins, biting her lip as he pulsed hard. He felt solid.

"Harder, don't stop baby, give it to me harder!" she screamed.

Speechless, his breathing increased, he raised his body, lifting her legs, fucking her harder and deeper. Moaning like he hadn't heard her before, he groaned with her.

"That's it, that feels so good," she moaned, her hands gripping her bed sheets as she orgasmed.

"Holy shit," he let out as he joined her in their moment of pleasure.

He continued to thrust into her as he finished; she found her breath as he slowed, still within her. Taking a deep sigh, he smiled.

"That was amazing," she grinned, looking flushed, her heart beating fast within her chest.

As they stopped he lay in between her runner's thighs, placing a kiss on her lips as if he was never going to let her go. Freya had never felt the sexual emotion she just experienced; she was in awe of him right now and wanted to stay in the moment forever. As he lifted out of her he lay beside her, cuddling her with their naked bodies amongst each other's.

"Freya, will you be my girlfriend?" he shyly asked, blushing.

She paused, smirking. "I will, Mr Jones, if you're allowed to date your colleagues, that is."

"What? You got the job?"

"I did." She paused with a beam, giggling.

"Well done, I knew you would." He kissed her on the forehead; they lay upon the bed cuddling naked until they fell asleep.

Freya woke feeling cold. Looking at the time, she had only slept for an hour. Climbing out of the bed she gazed upon Matt, who was sleeping deeply. She pulled the cover upon him, covering his bare butt, feeling lucky with how she finally had him in ways much more than she expected. Pulling on some shorts and a top, she blew out the candles, grabbed her phone and went downstairs. As she sat at the table sipping water she unlocked her phone to notice another two missed calls and another voicemail from Jack. She wondered why he was so eager to talk to her after no contact. She was in two minds about calling him but with it being the middle of the night she decided against it. Feeling like she was going behind Matt's back, she really needed to stop thinking about him, especially as she now officially had a boyfriend. She finished her water, listening to her voicemail.

"Hi Freya Are you alright? I'm tried calling you and you're not answering, I hope you're not ignoring me. I received your letter and cheque. You really didn't have to but thank you. I have some news I want to share with you but don't want to do it over the phone. Can we catch up when I'm home? Good luck for your marathon. I know you will smash it. Anyway, call me back. Bye…"

She listened to it twice. She hated the way he caused her stomach to do summersaults. Just his voice affected her in ways no other had. She had no defence against it, which now she wished she would.

Giving a sigh, she pushed it to the side and went back to bed where she tossed and turned as Matt slept next to her. Matt, her new boyfriend.

CHAPTER 14

26.2 Miles

As her eyes adjusted to the morning light she stretched out, noticing she was alone. The smell of breakfast filled the house and the chirping of birds was heard outside as they glided through the summer air, the sunshine beaming through the window. Finding herself smiling, she wanted to be in this minute forever; she felt completely in love with the moment. Feeling smug that she got to see him again today, she soon became saddened by the thought of having to prepare for her marathon in the next few days, knowing she would have to get out of bed and send him home soon if she wanted to succeed.

She hopped into the shower to rinse off the scent of sex which lingered upon her skin. As she reminisced about every feeling Matt gave her she found her knees buckling. Matt had touched her like no other which made her excited for more opportunities with him. She was confident he was her distraction from bad choices now she was no longer single. She felt like every recent negative moment was draining away along with the water as she rinsed herself off. A weight had lifted off her shoulders and her mind ran clear; she found herself singing to herself as she dressed and a skip in her step as she made her way to the kitchen.

"Morning, girlfriend." Matt turned, facing her, passing her a cup of tea with a kiss.

"Umm, morning, I could get used to this," she gushed.

He stood in nothing but his boxers. His solid athlete figure made her body ache for him as she looked into his dark green eyes. Her stomach flipped with desire.

"What?" he teased as she stood gawking at him.

"Nothing," she beamed, hiding her grin behind her mug. "Can I have you for breakfast?" she joked.

"Coming right up," he flirted, taking her mug out of her hand, taking her over his shoulder, carrying her back upstairs as she giggled with pleasure. "I don't actually know why you bothered getting dressed," he teased.

They failed to leave the house for the following week. Having spent most of it naked making love and fucking like rabbits in every inch of the house, they both had shared new sexual experiences with each other. Having always thought she was experienced in the bedroom, she was proven wrong by him now knowing she had literally been quite vanilla within her sexual experiences. Each time she became skin to skin with him she became excited at what was to come, knowing he was slowly breaking her in. Never failing to pleasure her. She was now becoming less and less afraid of love, querying whether she was falling for him as she felt so crazy in love right now.

It's Saturday in three days, she thought as Thursday morning crept by. Waking feeling tired and out of sorts from so much sex with her marathon being soon, she grew concerned. She didn't want to ask him to go so she could rest but she wanted to achieve her goal of crossing that finish line and knew she had to, much to her dismay.

"I'm going to go home today, let you prepare for your run and rest." He winked as they cuddled within the duvet. She looked up at him and sighed with slight relief and he kissed her forehead.

"You read my mind."

Matt finished his breakfast and covered his sexy body with clothes the first time since last week. Making her way to the car with him, the fresh air hit her; she inhaled as if it filled her with energy having been inside for so long.

"I'll see you at the finish line then." He suggested they have a few days apart.

"I miss you already," Freya admitted as she felt odd him leaving having become so attached to him and his body so quickly.

"Miss you," kissing her hand as he climbed into the car. She watched him drive off. Making her way back inside, she slumped onto the sofa before meal prepping for the next few days. She ensured she drank plenty and carb loaded with pastas, bread and protein ready to fuel her body for four hours of running plus a short one later. Each second of not being busy her mind drifted back to Matt; she wanted to talk to him and hear his voice. Feeling like a love-struck teenager, she continuously picked up her phone and placed it back down as she fought every impulse.

Distracting herself, she opened her laptop to check her emails and respond to her job offer. Having cancelled all her other planned interviews she skim read through well wishes from the companies she turned down. She opened her email and started to type.

Morning Mr Smith

I hope you are well, sorry for the delayed reply.

Firstly I would like to thank you for your job offer, it really made my day.

I would love to be part of your sports team in such a brilliant university and accept your fantastic offer.

I am free to start on the 29th as suggested and am looking forward to it.

Can I ask you to send me any requirements including uniform, equipment etc. to ensure I am prepared.

Thank you again.

Kind regards

Freya Bell

She closed her laptop. Gathering her running clothes, she went on to complete a short six-mile run and spent the day relaxing whilst texting Chloe, Nina and Louise, filling them up with her new boyfriend gossip. Planning to meet them at the finish line on Saturday too, she was excited for them to meet him properly as they planned a celebratory drink providing she survived.

Fully rested, fuelled and feeling ready Saturday's 6am alarm soon woke her with a startle. She had slept like a baby for the first time last night after Matt had allowed her to rest properly from their sexual antics. Nerves crept in at the thought of eating breakfast and getting ready for her first ever marathon. As it was due to be cooler this morning she dressed herself in layers which she planned to remove as she got warmer. Dressing in a sports bra, tank top and shorts she threw on a long-sleeve top which she didn't mind chucking off in the streets. She pinned her number onto her tops, put her favourite running shoes on, which were worn in perfectly, and she was ready. As she had prepared a playlist the night before she planned to relax on the train journey over, hoping her nerves would stay at bay. Unfortunately the train carriage being full of other runners made this hard as her stomach grew butterflies. As she looked around at the groups and couples she questioned as to why she had decided to run alone now, as some company may have made her feel less anxious. When nearing the station she received a message from Matt.

Morning gorgeous.

I haven't half missed you since I left <3

I hope you got some rest.

I'll be in the crowds cheering you on, see you at the finish line.

Xxxx

She smiled. Deciding not to reply she shut her phone back off to save her battery for her four hours of iTunes. She climbed off the train, following all the other runners and spectators to the shuttle bus over to the start line. As they arrived to the streets which were filling with thousands of people she now felt worried. *Can I actually run a marathon?* she thought to herself, having reminded herself she had never actually run more than 20 miles within her training; six extra miles was a lot. Her nerves were taking over as her body started to shake; her stomach churned and she felt sick. She took a deep breath over and over to calm herself as she checked she had her energy shots in her pockets and some Vaseline. She strapped her iPhone around her arm. With no going back now, she was as ready as she could be.

She stood in the corrals of runners which divided them into expected finishing times. She knew the gun was about to go. Scanning around, she saw so many faces, probably thousands. She didn't expect to see Matt, Chloe, Louise or Nina in the crowd, she didn't recognise anybody. As she stared at banners saying 'You're all winners', 'Go Daddy', 'You can do it', she heaved. Her palms felt sweaty, the waiting was making her feel worse, the seconds feeling like they were minutes. She just wanted to run, the anticipation eating at her. She pressed play on her running app and let her music start.

The gun cracked and everyone moved; her feet lifted off the ground so fast she knew she needed to slow down and find her pace as she saw others also sprinting off the start line as if they were racing Usain

Bolt. As she found her pace she ran to her music which helped her find her focus. She tried to shut everyone else out although the spectators were cheering so loudly it was difficult, the first mile being more difficult than she thought. Having been so used to running alone she felt claustrophobic and wanted space; she felt like she was running slower than normal. Her body warmed up into mile two, now having found her pace as others had also slowed. She was now feeling more comfortable. Making it into mile three the large groups of onlookers were behind her making her feel more in tune with her running. Time passed quickly as adrenaline filled her body and her music flowed filling her with enthusiasm. She heard spectators shouting, "Come on, you're nearly there!" As she reached mile five she laughed out loud. Her body felt strong as she passed queues at the toilet stations already. She looked on at numerous runners in wacky costumes which made the atmosphere more fun, although her heart sank a little every time a grey old man overtook her. She kept telling herself it's not a sprint it's a marathon, before her competitive side kicked in. The only battle she had today was with her body allowing her to get through the next three and a half hours as she admittedly felt exhausted.

As she chugged energy shots at water stations she felt pumped, having had enough to last a lifetime already. The first few tasted nice but having now reached the half-marathon marker she didn't fancy any more as her stomach started to feel queasy, although she knew she needed them to replenish her body. Her body started to become tired although her mental strength guided her, allowing her to carry on, having promised herself not to stop, knowing she would struggle to get her nine-mile pace back if she did. Her knee joints felt out of place as she felt herself working harder due to the dodging of plastic cups, foil packets and banana skins as she passed each station, the passing of subways and McDonald's were also making her feel hungry. She looked on at runners who were now struggling as she hit the 20-mile mark; collapsed runners were being seen by ambulance crews.

Every inch of her body now aching, she had started to feel chafing between her thighs and beneath her iPhone strap on her arm. Her skin feeling raw, eager to take it off, she resisted as her music was the only thing keeping her going plus the hordes of people who were appearing nearer the last miles. Having not passed 20 miles she needed some inspiration as she had suddenly hit the wall and her legs moved slower and slower. "Come on, you can do it," she whispered to herself.

"Come on, Freya!!" she heard being screamed next to her. She glanced aside to see Chloe, Nina and Louise cheering her on with a banner saying 'You'll Smash It!' She waved, smiling, hiding her pain and exhaustion. She pushed through the urge to stop and cry, forcing her legs to pump faster.

Mile 24 crept in as she slowed to a now ten-minute mile; she managed to rub some Vaseline between her thighs to help ease the chafing, her arm now raw and bleeding stung at every swing of her arms. Her body covered in sweat which was making it easier for her to burn from the sun which was now high in the sky on what turned out to be a very hot summer's day. The soles of her feet burning within her trainers, sure she could feel blisters all over her feet, her toenails feeling like they were going to fall off as she tried to adjust her feet within her trainer as she ran. She was so close to finishing. As her last few songs played upbeat into her ears she knew she could get through the wall in front of her. As she listened to every lyric and beat of the music she came in site of the 26th-mile marker, in complete pain and out of breath; her body felt like jelly. A moment of revelation hit her, knowing she was able to stop soon as huge crowds were at piling at the finishing line cheering everyone on. Tears rolled down her cheeks with the pure joy of having the end in sight.

She peered around in hope to see Matt through the crowds, in need of someone she knew to get her through the last minutes of agony. Then he emerged from the audience, her eyes squinting towards him as she double checked she wasn't hallucinating. His loud manly voice shouted, cheering her on, holding a sign saying 'You can do it Freya, I'm home'.

He stood before her in his shorts and polo shirt looking sexy as ever as she threw up in her mouth. Her mind span out of control into a tizzy like every time she saw him. *JACK!* she shouted to herself. He became closer as she hit the last stretch. Matt, appearing from the crowd, jumped over the barrier towards her to run the last few steps beside her, grabbing her hand and crossing the line with her as Jack watched on. From his sudden change in expression she assumed he was now aware of her relationship status. He clocked Chloe, Louise and Nina looking over at him as they followed Freya's eyeline, looking directly at him. In the hectic crowd she could hear nothing but cheering. A sudden feeling of panic surged through her body; she felt claustrophobic within the crowds. She let go of Matt's hand which she was still tightly holding onto and squeezed through the people ducking between them.

"Freya wait." She heard Matt behind her.

As she found some space allowing her to breathe she fell to the floor wrapped in her foil cape, feeling like she had been beaten up by Mike Tyson. Her mind foggy, her breathing erratic and her body in complete pain. Having not yet been hit with feelings of happiness from completing her first marathon she sat covered in sweat, blood and tears and said to herself, "I did it."

She spotted Matt through the crowd and shouted his name with the little energy she had remaining. He followed her voice and peeped through the wall of people between them.

"Well done, you did it! Are you alright?" He bent down towards her, looking concerned at the shade of white filling her face. "Freya!!" she heard bellowing towards her. She felt light headed, in a haze, unable to speak.

"Freya, here, have this." Jack bent down to her, holding her shoulder, handing her a sports drink and Boost bar as Matt rose, looking on with Chloe, Louise and Nina. She took it as she looked him in the face with confusion, feeling like a fool for feeling so weak.

She sipped the drink and took bites of the chocolate; she started to feel the sugar hit her, bringing her back to normality. Jack was there for her to lean on as she found herself again making sure she was OK.

"You did it, Freya, you should be so proud of yourself. I definitely couldn't do that and look at your arm," Chloe spoke as she rubbed her red raw, bleeding arm cut from her iPhone strap, removing it for her.

"Hi, I'm Jack," she could hear above her as she glimpsed up.

"Matt, Freya's boyfriend," she heard him respond with a tense voice, squirming at the word 'boyfriend' as it was said towards Jack, not wanted to see his reaction. Feeling awkward and embarrassed about her current situation, she didn't know what had come over her. As she felt better she stood up, her legs like jelly, her feet burning. She was eager to get them into some cold water.

"You back with us?" Matt asked as he brushed his hand against her sweaty face.

"Ye, sorry, I went funny. I feel better now. Thanks for the sugar, Jack," she spoke towards him, looking on at what she knew was his heartbroken expression. If only she was alone with him to express her feelings. She wished everyone would disappear to apologise; if only she had answered the phone and spoke to him she would have known he was going to be there rather than giving her a huge shock.

"Shall we go for a celebratory drink? I booked a table in a bar over there." Matt pointed.

"Ye, I need to sit and take my shoes off," she begged.

"Good with us," the girls responded.

"Jack, are you coming?" Freya suggested towards him, hoping Matt didn't mind.

"Actually I am going to head off, my parking ticket ends soon anyway," he awkwardly explained. "Nice to meet you all," he spoke towards the group.

"You guys go, I'll be a minute," Freya spoke towards Matt, Chloe, Louise and Nina, Matt not looking impressed as they walked towards the bar.

CHAPTER 15

Torn

Looking upon Jack's face, his emotions were written all over it. She could see what he felt without him having to say a word. He looked exactly how she felt the day he first left all those years ago. Completely heartbroken. Seeing her and Matt had hit him hard; she now felt awful for him having to find out this way. If only she had answered his call. She hated herself, having never wanted to hurt him. He looked into her eyes, knowing she was sorry as tears emerged and she fought them back. They could read each other without having to say anything.

The streets were still busy. She took his hand, slowly walking on her burning feet towards a bench. As she took each step she winced from the pain, breathing heavily through it, the relief hitting her as she took her shoes off.

"Well done, Freya, you did it, what you had always said you wanted to do, all that hard work paid off," he quietly congratulated her as he watched her, wishing he could take care of her.

"Thank you, I won't be doing one again anytime

soon," she mumbled as she tried to stretch her tight muscles, failing as it hurt too much. "Jack?" She paused, looking into his glossy eyes standing closely before him, her hand reaching to his cheek, caressing his soft clean-shaven face. His gaze looking down at her as he stood silent.

"Jack, I'm sorry, I messed up," she cried. "I'm sorry I haven't answered your calls or rang you back, I'm sorry you had to find out about Matt this way, I'm so sorry," she repeated as tears rolled down her face. Feeling apocalyptically exhausted, she lost all control of her emotion, tears falling so fast down her face she was ugly crying right in front of him, much to her humiliation.

"Freya, you don't have to apologise." He paused fighting back his emotions. "You weren't going to wait for me forever, I didn't expect you to. I'm happy you have found someone who treats you like you deserve. He seems nice, which I hate to admit," he stuttered.

"Ye he is," she spoke as she wiped away her tears.

"I just regret my choices now. If only I was here at the beginning of summer," he sighed.

"What do you mean?" she questioned.

He placed the sign which he was holding onto her lap as he failed to find the answer to her question. His happy ending now not so happy. Confused, she looked at him and looked down at it as she read it, her tear drops landing on the paper smudging the handwritten words 'You can do it Freya, I'm home'.

Looking back at him she knew what he was saying. Her heart sank, she felt sick, she had been waiting a lifetime for him. Why now?

He read her expression as a tear fell down his cheek as he watched her heart shatter. She slumped into the bench with cries streaming down her face.

"You're home, aren't you? Home for good?" Her voice quivered.

"Ye," he stammered, lost for words. "Yes, I am." He shrugged his shoulders as she placed her head in her hands.

His strong arm reached around her, comforting her. She leaned her head against him as they fell silent for a minute. The silence between them felt like forever, neither of them knowing what to say.

Breaking the quietness, Jack stood from the bench, looking down at her as she rose. "You best go back, they are waiting to celebrate with you."

His eyes glistened, holding back further tears like any man would do, choked on his words as he went to speak.

"Freya, I see nobody but you. I always have and I've waited this long. I can wait some more," he whispered in her ear. He gave her a hug; she squeezed him tightly back, never wanting to let go, unsure if she would ever get to again. He treasured the moment, breathing in her scent, holding her, fighting every urge not to kiss her. As they stood in the moment Matt appeared around the corner, appearing in Jack's eyeline, looking for her. As he saw them he looked at Jack, him looking back at him. He turned back round, moving out of sight. Freya unaware, he let her go, making space between them, looking up at him as he wiped away her tears.

"Go on, I'll see you soon," he insisted as he let her

go. He kissed her on the cheek and walked away. She stood struggling to find any words, saying completely nothing as she felt her every emotion crumble within her. Every step he took hurt as he drew further away. Her body ached, her feet burning, her thighs raw, she felt battered, mentally confused and broken. Her heart was aching for Jack but also for Matt. As he was nearly out of sight he looked back at her and smiled. She felt torn.

ABOUT THE AUTHOR

As a young child I grew up all over Leicestershire. Having never settled into school until the secondary years my academic life never opened up a career path that I truly wished to follow. I then met my childhood sweetheart at the age of 14 where my life soon revolved around him, until his career choice took him to join the army. I then spent my time wishing the school years away and socialising with my friends as any normal teenager would.

At the young age of 18 my first son was born, bringing my boyfriend home from the army. We're now 15 years on, have been married for eight years and have three sons and one daughter. We enjoy a very busy life of juggling work, school, hobbies and parenting.

Between each child I have tried several careers from childcare, travel sales, bar work – none of which felt like the perfect career. I finally chose to step back and enjoy time at home as a mum. This allowed me the time to finally write down the short stories which had filled my mind for the past few years.

In January 2019 my imagination brought me to Freya, whom some would say is my alter ego. Within the babies' nap times and quiet evenings Freya's story soon became long enough to call a book. I have thoroughly fallen in love with Freya and her life's journey; she is now the main character of *Spontaneously Reckless* with the works of sequel *Spontaneously Torn* being in place.

Printed in Great Britain
by Amazon

33204950R00139